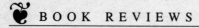 **BOOK REVIEWS**

Here's what people are saying:

A satisfying plot, this book is sure to be popular.

from SCHOOL LIBRARY JOURNAL

This approachable story of contemporary life deals sensibly with real issues and concerns. It should make popular, worthwhile reading.

from KIRKUS

CASSIE

ESPECIALLY FOR GIRLS® Presents

CASSIE

A NOVEL BY

MARILYN KAYE

GULLIVER BOOKS

HARCOURT BRACE JOVANOVICH
PUBLISHERS

San Diego   New York   London

This book is a presentation of **Especially for Girls,**® Weekly Reader Books. Weekly Reader Books offers book clubs for children from preschool through high school. For further information write to: **Weekly Reader Books,** 4343 Equity Drive, Columbus, Ohio 43228.

Published by arrangement with Harcourt Brace Jovanovich, Publishers. Especially for Girls and Weekly Reader are federally registered trademarks of Field Publications.

Library of Congress Cataloging-in-Publication Data
Kaye, Marilyn.
    Cassie.
    "Gulliver books."
    Summary: Thirteen-year-old Cassie, bemoaning the fact that her family cannot afford designer clothes or exotic vacations, is enchanted with her rich new friend Dana, until an incident makes her see Dana in a different light.
    [1. Friendship—Fiction. 2. Wealth—Fiction. 3. Shoplifting—Fiction]
I. Title. II. Series: Kaye, Marilyn. Sisters.
PZ7.K2127Cas 1987   [Fic]   87-11944
ISBN 0-15-200421-1
ISBN 0-15-200422-X (pbk.)

Frontispiece by Roberta Ludlow
Designed by Julie Durrell
Printed in the United States of America
    C D E

For Corinne Van Houten and Marc Anselme

But barbie was in a rush. "I better run—I don't want to get four days' detention. I'll see you at lunch."

She dashed off, and Cassie continued down the hall toward her locker. The halls were getting crowded now as more students arrived, and she was stopped several

CASSIE

and started down the hall toward their homeroom.

"How's the Pep Club?" Julie asked.

"Pretty good," Cassie replied. "We got a lot of the seventh graders to join." Not her own kid sister, though. She'd tried to get Daphne involved with the Pep Club,

1

"HEY, YOU GUYS—look at this." Cassie entered the kitchen where her two younger sisters were playing Scrabble. She held an open magazine in front of them and indicated a picture.

Daphne raised her eyes from the board. "It's very nice," she said politely.

Phoebe leaned over to take a look. "It's just a raincoat."

Cassie snatched the magazine back. "It's not just a raincoat, you ignorant child. It's an English Mist."

"What's an English Mist?" Daphne asked.

Cassie pulled a chair up to the table and sat down between them.

"Watch it," Phoebe warned, "you almost upset the board."

Cassie ignored her and directed her remarks to

1

Daphne. "Everyone's got an English Mist. Every girl in the eighth grade has an English Mist. Except me."

"Oh, c'mon," Daphne remonstrated. "I can't believe *everyone* in the eighth grade has an English Mist."

Cassie shrugged. "Everyone who's anyone. Haven't you seen them? They must be wearing them in the seventh grade, too."

"I don't know. I guess I never noticed."

"What's the big deal?" Phoebe asked. "You've got a raincoat. We all do. Mom bought all four of us raincoats at that sale last year, remember?"

Cassie scowled at her. "I know I have a raincoat. But it's not an English Mist. And Mom won't let me buy one." She examined her sisters' faces for any trace of sympathy. Phoebe was looking at the letters on her wooden rack, tugging at her stringy, light brown hair. Her plump face showed no evidence of concern for Cassie's plight. She thought she saw a trace of anxiety in Daphne's dark eyes, but . . .

"*E-X-C-I-T-E*." With one hand, Daphne pushed her glasses back up her nose and with the other arranged the letters on the board.

"Gee," Phoebe murmured in awe, "you got a double word score and that's a triple under the *X*." Rapidly she began figuring on a pad of paper sitting by her elbow. "That's sixty-two points."

Cassie decided to give her sisters one last chance to show some support. "You just don't know what it's like," she said passionately. "People see my raincoat and they look at me with pity in their eyes! It's so depressing."

The despair in her voice must have touched something in Daphne's sensitive heart. While Phoebe concentrated on making a word from her letters, Daphne reached for the magazine and studied the picture.

"This doesn't look any different from our raincoats, Cassie. Except for the color, of course."

"Oh, the color's not important," Cassie explained. "English Mists come in a lot of different colors. But look," she said, using her finger to indicate the different parts of the coat, "the collar's rounder than mine, and the buttons are bigger. And see the stitching here? Our raincoats don't have stitching like that."

Daphne squinted at the picture. "You'd have to look really close to see the difference. Do girls actually stare at each other's raincoats that hard?"

"No, of course not," Cassie said. "But everyone who has an English Mist carries it open across her arm so the label shows."

"Al-right!" Phoebe exclaimed. She placed her squares on the board. "*L-A-B-E-L*. Hey, Cassie—why don't you just get a label and sew it inside your own coat? Then everyone will think it's a real English Mist."

Cassie couldn't help grinning. "That's what Barbie said I should do. She thinks I should go into a department store and try on an English Mist. Then, when I'm alone in the dressing room, I could cut out the label."

Daphne looked dubious. "Wouldn't that be stealing?"

"I don't know. I guess so. I mean, even though I wouldn't actually be stealing the coat, without the label the coat probably wouldn't be worth all that much." She sighed deeply. "Oh, I *wish* I could talk Mom into getting me one."

"Getting you one what?" A lanky, short-haired figure strolled into the kitchen and headed for the refrigerator.

"An English Mist raincoat. Don't you want one? Everyone at school has an English Mist."

"That's a perfectly good reason *not* to get one."

"Oh, Lydia," Cassie groaned. She should have known better than to even mention wanting something everyone else had to her one-year-older sister. If everyone wore flats, Lydia wore sneakers. If everyone else was into skirts, Lydia refused to wear anything but pants.

Lydia got an apple from the refrigerator. She took a noisy bite and joined her sisters at the table. "Who's winning?"

"Daphne," Phoebe muttered. "Personally, I think I should get extra points because I'm younger."

"Only a year," Daphne reminded her.

"Yeah, but I think your vocabulary doubles when you get into junior high."

Cassie got up and left the room. Nobody understood—at least, nobody in her family. Didn't they know what it was like when all your friends had something and you didn't? They didn't even seem to care about things like that. Of course, Lydia was weird. And Phoebe was too young. As for Daphne—well, Daphne was so serious. All she cared about was school and artsy stuff and writing her poems.

Barbie understood. She felt sorry for Cassie. But that wasn't much comfort. Cassie didn't want sympathy— not even from her best friend. All she wanted was an English Mist.

She wandered into the living room, where her mother was sitting in an armchair, a stack of papers on her lap.

"What are you doing, Mom?"

Her mother flashed her a brief smile before scrawling something in red on a paper. "Grading papers."

"What are they about?" Cassie asked, trying to sound very interested.

"*Hamlet*," her mother murmured.

Cassie tried to think of something to say about Hamlet, but all she knew was that he'd had a play written about him.

"Are the papers good?"

"Not bad. Definitely an improvement over the last set."

"I'll bet that's because you're such a good teacher," Cassie said brightly.

With that, her mother actually looked up. "Okay, Cassie—what's going on?"

Cassie gazed at her with wide-eyed innocence. "Huh?"

"Darling, I know you, and you're trying to butter me up for something."

Cassie smiled sheepishly. "I was just wondering if I could borrow on my allowance."

Mrs. Gray closed her eyes. "Oh, Cass, you're not going to start up again about that raincoat, are you?"

One look at her mother's face told Cassie it was a hopeless cause. Of course, there was still her father . . .

"And don't start bugging your father about it either."

Cassie looked up, startled. Was she *that* transparent? "Where is Daddy, anyway?" It suddenly dawned on her that she hadn't seen him all that Sunday.

"He's at the newspaper. One of his reporters is sick, and he has to work on that special series they're doing."

"What special series?"

Her mother looked aggravated. "Cassie, don't you even read your own father's newspaper? They've been running a series on troubled youth."

"Oh." Cassie wondered if any of the youth had the troubles she had.

Her mother lifted the papers off her lap and put them on an end table. "Your father should be home shortly. I'd better get dinner started, and I think it's your turn to help."

"Okay," Cassie replied glumly.

Mrs. Gray gazed at her keenly. "Look, Cass, I'm sorry about the raincoat. Believe it or not, I *do* remember what it was like when I was your age. I know how important it can be to keep up with your peers. But honey, we don't have that kind of money, and even if we did . . ." She paused, searching for the right words. "I don't want to encourage that kind of attitude."

"What kind of attitude?"

"Oh, keeping up with the Joneses, that sort of materialism. I want you girls to have solid values and realize how very lucky you are. You've got a nice home and plenty of food, parents and sisters who love you . . ."

"Well, everyone's got that," Cassie objected.

"Oh, no they don't," her mother stated firmly. "You really should read your father's series."

Cassie reached for the newspaper lying on the coffee table, but was stopped by her mother's next words.

"After you help me get dinner going."

Cassie scowled. But her mother ignored the expression and headed toward the kitchen. Reluctantly, Cassie pulled herself up and followed her in.

"Okay, girls, time to set the table," Mrs. Gray called out.

"But we're in the middle of a game," Phoebe protested.

"Then transfer it to the living room. I want dinner on the table when your father comes home. He's had a rough weekend."

Gingerly, Phoebe and Daphne lifted the board, trying not to upset the letter formations on it. Lydia directed the operation.

"Daphne, you're leaning to the left! Fee, don't bump into the chair!"

While this was going on, the phone rang. "I'll get it," Cassie said. In her rush to grab the phone, she brushed Daphne's arm. A dozen or so wooden tiles dropped to the floor.

"Cassie, look what you did!" Phoebe yelled.

"Sorry," Cassie muttered as she reached for the phone. What was all that garbage her mother had just been handing her about loving families? Forget it.

"Hello?"

"Hi, it's me."

"Oh, hi Barbie." Cassie caught her mother's eye. She grimaced and nodded. "Look, I can't talk right now. We're getting dinner ready."

"Okay, then I'll talk fast. Guess what?"

"What?"

"Someone moved into the Dibbley mansion today. I was walking past and I saw the moving vans."

That *was* news. The Dibbley mansion was the biggest, fanciest house in Cedar Park, and it had been vacant for years. The Dibbleys had been the richest people in town. They'd moved away ages ago.

"Did you see the people who moved in?"

"I saw a girl—she looked about eighteen."

"Cassandra!" Her mother was getting what they all called "the look."

"Barbie, I gotta go. I'll call you later, okay?"

"No, we're going to my grandmother's for dinner. I'll see you at school."

Cassie hung up the phone. She wondered who could have bought that mansion. Maybe it was somebody famous. She was about to announce Barbie's news to the others when the back door opened and her father entered.

"Good evening, ladies. How are all my lovely women doing?" His voice was breezy, but he looked tired.

There was a chorus of *Hi, Dad*.

Mrs. Gray hurried over and gave him a kiss. "Honey, you must be exhausted. Dinner will be ready in just a few minutes."

Mr. Gray sat down at the table. "I'm beat," he admitted.

"The series?" Mrs. Gray asked.

Mr. Gray nodded. "Yeah, it's a pretty draining experience. Intellectually *and* emotionally."

"Are you talking about the troubled youth series?" Daphne asked. "I read the first part today. It was really interesting."

Lydia nodded fervently. "Yeah. Right on target."

Cassie was just going to ask what it was about, but that would be admitting she hadn't read it yet.

Mr. Gray sighed. "You know, you girls are really

lucky. You wouldn't believe the problems some kids your age have."

"Like what?" Phoebe asked.

Mr. Gray's normally cheerful face looked sad. "Oh, drugs, abuse, general neglect. . . . There are a lot of unloved kids in this world."

"Don't they have parents?" Cassie asked.

Mr. Gray managed a smile. "Not all kids have exceptionally fantastic parents like you girls."

"Well, this exceptionally fantastic mother and her daughters had all better get their acts in gear or nobody's going to get fed tonight. Cassie, will you get the salad stuff out of the refrigerator? And somebody get that magazine off the table."

Cassie hadn't realized she'd left it there. Before she could pick it up, her father glanced at the open page. And she couldn't pass up the opportunity.

"Isn't that a pretty coat?" she asked casually. She kept her voice as soft as possible, but could still feel her mother glaring at her.

Her father peered at the picture and read the advertisement out loud. " 'The original English Mist. For men and women. Twelve colors, all sizes. And it's yours for only $135.' "

"Cassie!" her mother said sharply. "I said get the magazine off the table."

But her father grinned at her. "Yes, it's a beautiful coat. Wish *I* could afford one."

His knowing eyes made Cassie realize once again how transparent she was. But she couldn't help returning the grin. "Yeah. Me too."

2

ANYONE WHO WANTS a ride to school better be down here in five minutes!"

The sound of her mother's voice forced Cassie to remove her eyes from the mirror and glance out the window. The morning mist had turned into a steady drizzle, and Cassie moaned. She glanced back at her reflection. Her hair looked great now, the soft, blonde waves tumbling down her shoulders. But the second her hair realized what was going on outside—boom! Major frizz.

"Cassie, c'mon, hurry up!" Lydia ran a comb through her hair without even bothering to look into the mirror and dashed out of the bedroom.

Well, rain had one compensation. They would get a ride to school. Quickly, Cassie outlined her lips in dark pink, applied a lighter pink lipstick, and smeared on some lip gloss.

When she finally made her way down to the kitchen, the usual morning activity was winding up. Her sisters were wolfing down cereal, her father was gulping the last of his coffee, and her mother was watching the clock.

"Girls, you've got exactly ninety seconds. At that point, I'm taking off—whether you're in the car or not."

Phoebe paused between mouthfuls. "My health teacher says we have to eat slowly if we're going to digest properly. Besides, I don't need a ride. Linn's mother is picking me up."

Her mother smiled benignly. "Then you just go right ahead and digest all you want. But the rest of you—"

"I'm off," Mr. Gray said. He took a last gulp of coffee, kissed his wife hastily, and threw a general kiss in the direction of his daughters before heading toward the door.

"I just want some juice," Cassie said.

Her father paused at the door and looked at her. There were creases of concern on his forehead. "Pumpkin, you should eat something. You're not developing one of those adolescent eating disorders, are you? We've got an article on that in our series."

"I'm fine, Dad," Cassie assured him. "I'm just not all that hungry."

Her father sighed. "I guess I just can't get this series off my mind. All these kids with so many problems . . ." He was still shaking his head as he walked out the door.

Lydia started to hand Cassie the juice carton, but then

paused to look at it. "Are there any chemicals in this juice?"

Daphne looked up. "Why would there be chemicals in orange juice?"

"Preservatives," Lydia said. "And you wouldn't believe what they do to our bodies. Have you any idea what goes into hot dogs, for example?"

Mrs. Gray snatched the orange juice carton from her and handed it to Cassie. "Honestly, Lydia, do you think I'd give my daughters something unhealthy to drink?"

"You never know," Lydia said darkly. "They sneak those chemicals in. You never know what's in that stuff."

Cassie examined the carton. "Do chemicals have a lot of calories?"

Daphne adjusted her glasses and leaned over to look at the carton. " 'One hundred percent natural orange juice,' " she read. "I think it's okay."

"Thirty seconds," Mrs. Gray announced.

Somehow, by the end of that half-minute, Cassie, Lydia, and Daphne were all in the car. On the way to Cedar Park Junior High, Cassie remembered Barbie's news of the evening before.

"Guess what? Somebody finally bought the Dibbley mansion. Barbie saw people moving in yesterday."

"I always thought that house looked like a castle," Daphne said dreamily. "I wonder what kind of people moved in."

"Whoever they are," Mrs. Gray remarked, "they must be very wealthy. The last I heard, they were asking close to two million for that house."

Two million. Cassie tried to think of what that would look like written out. Was it six zeros or nine?

"Two million," Daphne said in awe. "Wow, maybe they're movie stars or something like that."

"Two million," Lydia echoed, but her tone was different. "That's disgusting. With all the homeless people in this world, spending that kind of money on shelter is disgusting. It's . . . it's conspicuous consumption."

"What's conspicuous consumption?" Cassie asked.

Mrs. Gray glanced into the rear view mirror. "It's like when people buy raincoats they don't need just because of the label."

Cassie rolled her eyes and slumped in her seat.

Lydia's eyes were shining. "I think people should get back to basics. Cut the frills, get rid of the nonessentials in their lives. People would be a lot happier."

"Sounds good to me," Mrs. Gray said cheerfully. "We could start with your stereo. I mean, who needs a stereo? A little radio would be just as good."

Lydia blinked. "Well, that wasn't exactly what I had in mind. . . ."

Mrs. Gray pulled up in front of the junior high. "Have a good day, girls," she sang out. "Don't consume anything too conspicuously."

The girls raced through the rain into the building. There weren't too many people at school yet. Cassie headed directly to her locker, hoping to get rid of her raincoat before too many kids saw her.

"Cassie!"

She turned to see Barbie running toward her. "Hi! What are you doing here so early?"

Barbie made a face. "I've got detention for two days. For being late last week. You remember, when I met Darryl before homeroom last week?"

Cassie remembered. Barbie had met her new boy-friend behind the gym. And they sort of lost track of the time. She tried to look sympathetic, but it wasn't easy. At least Barbie had a steady boyfriend now. It was probably worth two days' detention.

Barbie looked up at the hallway clock. "I have to report to the cafeteria in one minute. But I had to find you first. Guess what? I saw her!"

"Who?" Cassie asked.

"The girl who moved into the Dibbley mansion!"

"Where'd you see her?"

"Here! She's a student!"

"You're kidding!" Cassie exclaimed. "I thought you said she was older."

"Well, she definitely looks older. But I just saw her in the principal's office, and she's being registered for the eighth grade."

"What does she look like?" Cassie couldn't even imagine what a girl whose family had two million dollars would look like.

But Barbie was in a rush. "I better run—I don't want to get four days' detention. I'll see you at lunch."

She dashed off, and Cassie continued down the hall toward her locker. The halls were getting crowded now as more students arrived, and she was stopped several times by friends. It always made her feel good walking down the halls and realizing how many people knew her and wanted to talk to her. She knew she was popular, and she liked that. She might not be in the very best crowd—that was made up of the superrich kids, the country club set, who lived on the Hill, where the

Dibbley mansion was. But she was definitely in the next-best, and that was pretty good.

By the time Cassie reached her locker, there were only a few minutes left before the bell, and she hastily worked her combination. As soon as she got the door open, she thrust her raincoat inside.

"Hi, Cassie."

The girl with the locker next to hers had just arrived. "Hi, Julie."

Julie Bradshaw was in her homeroom. Cassie didn't know her very well—she was a "Deb." The Debs were a sort of club, a group of girls who belonged to the Cedar Park Country Club. When they turned seventeen, they'd all be debutantes, and their pictures would be in Cassie's father's newspaper.

She noticed that Julie didn't put her raincoat in the locker. She kept it draped casually over her arm—and no wonder. The English Mist label was clearly visible for all the school to see.

The two girls closed their lockers at the same time and started down the hall toward their homeroom.

"How's the Pep Club?" Julie asked.

"Pretty good," Cassie replied. "We got a lot of the seventh graders to join." Not her own kid sister, though. She'd tried to get Daphne involved with the Pep Club, but for some crazy reason Daphne had suddenly decided to join the Creative Writing Club instead. She'd never understand her sister.

"I wish I could be more active," Julie said. "But the Debs do volunteer work at the hospital, and I just don't have time for anything else."

Cassie nodded. Personally, she didn't think hospital volunteer work sounded too exciting, but if that was the price you had to pay to be a Deb, she wouldn't mind. . . .

The bell rang just as they entered their homeroom. Cassie took her seat next to Alison Newmark, a Pep Club friend. They only had a minute to exchange hasty greetings before the homeroom teacher took roll. This was immediately followed by the bells signifying the intercom.

"Good morning," came the voice through the speaker. "May I have your attention for the daily announcements."

As usual, no one paid much attention to the daily announcements. So when the classroom door opened and the principal's secretary walked in with a strange girl, everyone turned to look.

The girl was definitely worth looking at. Cassie couldn't take her eyes off her. The teacher held a whispered conference with the secretary, so Cassie had time to get a good long look at this amazing stranger.

She looked like someone who might be on the cover of a fashion magazine. And not just *Seventeen*, or one of those other teenage magazines—more like *Vogue*. Her hair was streaked blonde, styled in a way Cassie had seen only in magazines, not on real people—longer on the sides, with curly side-swept bangs. And she wore makeup—not just a little lipstick and blush like the rest of the girls, but real eye makeup with heavy blue liner circling her eyes.

But it was her dress that really stood out. Most of the girls at Cedar Park Junior High wore jeans or skirts.

This girl wore an elegant black dress that fitted snugly. Not so tight that it looked trashy, but just tight enough so that it looked like it was made for her. Around her neck was a string of pearls that Cassie suspected just might be real. And she wore heels—not skinny funny-looking ones like some of the punk girls wore. Elegant heels.

"Who's that?" asked the boy sitting on Cassie's other side.

"Don't know," Cassie whispered back.

The boy gave her a grin. "Personally, I prefer *natural* blondes."

Cassie smiled back and tossed her head so her natural blonde hair swept across her back. It was the first time that term that Gary Stein had actually spoken to her. And she'd had her eyes on him for weeks.

The secretary left, and the teacher addressed the class. "This is Dana Cunningham, who has just moved here from, uh . . ."

"Chicago," the girl uttered in a bored voice.

"Yes, Chicago. Dana, why don't you take a seat there."

If Cassie had been Dana, she would have felt weird, knowing everyone was staring at her. But Dana looked very calm as she took her seat with cool confidence.

Cassie surreptitiously glanced around the room. Everyone was looking at Dana. She noticed that Julie Bradshaw and Nancy Ellison were whispering. They're probably wondering if she's Deb material, Cassie thought. From the look of that dress and the pearls, she was probably rich enough. But she didn't look like anyone else at Cedar Park Junior High.

By third period, everyone knew about Dana Cunningham, and rumors were flying fast.

"She's the one who moved into the Dibbley mansion," Barbie said as she and Cassie sat down at a table in the cafeteria.

"I asked her where she lived in Chicago," Alison reported. "They're from that section called the Gold Coast—you know, those fancy apartment buildings where the millionaires live."

"And she just got back from the Riviera," Barbie added. "That's what someone told me."

Remembering Daphne's comment that morning, Cassie asked, "Are her parents famous? Like movie stars?"

Two friends from the Pep Club, Amy and Susan, plunked their trays down at the table. They obviously guessed who everyone was talking about.

"I don't think they're movie stars," Amy said, "but I heard someone say her mother's a real fashion model."

"And I think her father's some kind of jet-set business tycoon," offered Susan.

"Look—there she is," Barbie whispered, unnecessarily. The cafeteria was so noisy no one could have heard her. Besides, practically half the room was looking at Dana Cunningham.

She was sitting with Julie and Nancy and a couple of other Deb girls. She didn't seem to be saying much, just sitting and picking at her food while the Debs chattered.

"I wonder if she'd be interested in the Pep Club," Amy murmured.

Cassie shrugged, but privately, she didn't think Dana looked like the type. There was something about her that was so sophisticated and different. Cassie just couldn't picture her doing cheers in the football stands.

"There she goes," Barbie said. Cassie watched as Dana left her group and strolled toward the exit. She even seemed to walk differently from everyone else.

"I think she's in your Spanish class," Alison told Cassie. "Don't you have Senorita Del Sordo, fifth period?"

"Yeah," Cassie said. "How come you know so much about her? Did you guys talk after homeroom?"

"A little," Alison said. "Actually, she wasn't very friendly."

Cassie could believe that. Dana didn't look like the kind of person who would be very friendly. But she was interesting—definitely interesting. And Cassie had to admit she was looking forward to seeing her in Spanish.

But she saw her sooner than that. After leaving her friends, Cassie had a few minutes before her next class and went to the restroom to fix her hair. From experience, she knew that the restroom across from the gym would be the least crowded at lunchtime, and she was right. There was only one other girl in it.

But Dana Cunningham wasn't fixing her hair. She was leaning against the back wall, and she was smoking a cigarette.

Cassie tried not to look shocked. She knew there was a group of girls, punk types, who smoked cigarettes in the bathrooms. But Dana didn't look punk.

"Hello," Dana said.

"Hi," Cassie replied. She took out her makeup bag, removed her brush, and began working on her hair. In the mirror, she could see the girl watching her.

"You're in my homeroom, aren't you? Want a cigarette?"

"Yeah," Cassie said. Seeing the girl reach into her purse, she hastily added, "No! I mean, yeah, you're in my homeroom, but no thanks, I don't want a cigarette."

Dana smiled. "In France, everyone smokes."

"Really?" Cassie couldn't help but give her an admiring look. Not that she'd ever wanted to smoke. But Dana looked so cool and elegant. . . . "I'm Cassie Gray," she said.

"Dana Cunningham," the girl replied. She tossed the cigarette into a toilet. "See you around." And she sauntered out.

She's glamorous, Cassie thought. Then she looked at herself in the mirror. The image that usually pleased her didn't please her at all.

When she went into her Spanish class, she didn't see Dana. She did see Gary Stein, though, who stopped by her desk. "Did you get that assignment done for today? It was pretty rough."

Cassie nodded. "Most of it. I thought it was pretty rough, too."

He nodded in agreement, then proceeded on to his desk. Cassie looked after him thoughtfully. Definitely cute.

Senorita Del Sordo entered, the bell rang, and class started. Alison must have been wrong, Cassie thought. Dana wasn't in the room.

But ten minutes into class, the elegant girl walked in. "Sorry I'm late," she said to the teacher. "It's my first day, and I was a little lost."

Again, the whole class was looking at her, but Dana

didn't seem to mind at all. The teacher checked her name on a list and indicated a seat toward the back. Dana walked past Cassie and their eyes met. The new girl gave her a slight smile, and for some reason, it made Cassie feel good.

After school, she met Barbie on the steps outside and recounted her experiences with Dana.

"She was *smoking*? That's gross," Barbie said.

"But she was in France, and everyone smokes there," Cassie explained.

"Well, she's in Cedar Park, Illinois, now," Barbie said. "Do you have any idea how much detention you can get for smoking in the bathrooms?"

Cassie was about to admit she had no idea at all, when Barbie suddenly said, "Look!"

Cassie looked. A car was pulling up to the front of the school. Actually, it wasn't a car at all—it was a limousine, a big white one. It stopped at the entrance and a man in a uniform got out.

And there was Dana, tripping lightly down the steps, looking neither to the left nor the right. The uniformed driver held the back door open as she got into the car.

Cassie and Barbie watched in silence as the car pulled away. And then, in unison, they uttered the only remark possible under the circumstances: *"Wow."*

3

S HE'S SO ELEGANT," Cassie said as she passed the salad bowl to Daphne. "You must have seen her in the halls. She's got streaked hair, sort of like Mom's, but more blonde. And she was wearing a black dress and real pearls."

"How could you tell they were real?" Lydia asked.

"Oh, you can tell," Cassie said loftily. "Real pearls have a special rosy glow." She'd read that somewhere, so she figured it must be true.

"Maybe I did see her," Daphne mused. "I thought she was a new teacher. Is she really in the eighth grade?"

"It must be hard for her, coming here in the middle of the term," Mrs. Gray commented. "I'm surprised her parents didn't move here earlier, so she could start school on time."

"Her father's an international jet-set businessman and

her mother's a high-fashion model," Cassie continued. "They lived on the Gold Coast in Chicago."

"I think I saw her leaving the cafeteria with the Debs," Lydia said. "She looks like a typical rich snob."

Phoebe paused between bites of chicken pie to address Lydia. "You shouldn't judge a book by its cover."

"Wow, that's really profound, Fee," Lydia replied.

"She might be shy," Daphne said thoughtfully. "Sometimes when you're shy, people think you're a snob. There's a girl in my homeroom who was in my class at Eastside Elementary. And she told me she used to think I was a snob! I couldn't believe it."

Neither could Cassie. Daphne was the furthest thing from a snob she could imagine. As for Dana . . .

"Well, if she *is* a snob, she's probably got a perfect right to be one. She got picked up from school by a limousine. And she spent the summer on the Riviera."

"You certainly know a lot about this girl," her mother said. "Did you spend time with her?"

"Not really," Cassie admitted. "I just heard a lot about her from everyone else. But I talked to her for a minute in the restroom, and I thought she was kind of friendly." She didn't mention the smoking.

"I hope you were nice to her. She's probably having a hard time adjusting, and she'll need a friend."

"Oh, sure, I was nice to her." Cassie sighed. "But I kind of doubt we'll be friends. She'll probably get involved with Julie and Nancy and—"

Phoebe, who had been concentrating on her food, interrupted. "Hey—where's Daddy?"

"He's still at the office," Mrs. Gray told her. "He won't be home till late."

"How come?" Lydia asked.

Phoebe looked anxious. "You guys aren't getting a divorce, are you?"

Her mother looked startled. "Of course not. Whatever gave you that idea?"

"Well, in this book I'm reading, this girl's parents are getting divorced, and at the beginning the father started coming home late every day." She paused, then added dramatically, "He was seeing another woman."

"Your father couldn't handle another woman," Mrs. Gray retorted dryly. "He's got all he can manage right here."

"How come he's working late all the time?" Daphne asked.

"It's that series. He's very involved in it."

Cassie was only half-listening. "What series?"

"Cassie, I told you. It's a ten-part series for the Sunday paper on troubled adolescents."

Lydia grinned. "Cassie thinks troubled adolescents are girls who don't have English Mist raincoats."

Cassie made a face at her. She knew perfectly well what troubled adolescents were. She just didn't know any.

"Hey, Mom," she asked, "where *is* the Riviera, anyway?"

Cassie couldn't wait to see what Dana would be wearing the next day at school. But the bell rang in homeroom, the teacher took roll, the morning announcements came over the intercom, and still no Dana. The period was half over before she finally walked in.

"I'm terribly sorry," Cassie heard her say earnestly

to the teacher. "I overslept. I have this jet lag, you see . . ."

The teacher didn't look terribly sympathetic. "Did you bring a note?"

Dana looked appropriately apologetic. "No, I was so anxious to get here as soon as I could, I didn't think of it."

"Well, since this is your first week here, I won't send you to the office. But please try to get over your jet lag before this happens again."

"Oh, I will," Dana said. But as she turned away from the teacher, she looked directly at Cassie and winked.

Was she winking at her? Cassie wondered. She wasn't sure if she should wink back or not. But she did manage a smile as Dana walked past to her seat.

"Look at that outfit," Alison whispered.

Cassie had been looking ever since Dana had walked into the room. This time she wore a long, slinky, soft sweater—Cassie suspected it was real cashmere—over a matching skirt that came almost to her ankles. It was the new length. Cassie had just seen it in a fashion magazine. Of course, nobody in Cedar Park was wearing anything like that.

When the bell rang, signifying the end of homeroom, she expected to see Dana engulfed by Julie and Nancy. But Dana rose languidly and ambled to the door alone. Out in the hallway, Cassie found herself walking next to her. Dana smiled at her. Cassie tried to think of something to say. "I love your outfit."

Dana seemed pleased. "I bought it in Paris. French clothes are so much nicer than American, don't you think? I mean, they're made to really fit."

Cassie nodded in agreement. "Oh, I know what you mean."

"Have you been to Paris?"

"Well, no, not exactly, but I've read about it."

Dana looked at her appraisingly. "You know, you could wear this style. It's not for everyone, of course, but you're tall enough, and you've got the right kind of figure."

Cassie smiled happily. Of course, there was no way in the world her mother would ever let her have an outfit like that, but it was nice to know she could wear it if she could get it.

As they moved through the crowded hallway, Dana wrinkled her nose. "It's so crowded here. And it's cold."

Cassie agreed. The fall weather had taken a sudden dip, and apparently the school heating system hadn't caught up.

"It was so warm on the Riviera this summer," Dana murmured.

"Were you on the French Riviera or the Italian Riviera?" Cassie asked, mentally thanking her mother for her explanation of geography.

"The French, of course."

"Of course," Cassie said, not sure why. "You must have been on the beach a lot. You've got a great tan," she added enviously. Her own had faded weeks ago.

"Oh, sure, I was on the beach every day." She gave Cassie a sidelong glance. "We bathe topless there, you know."

Cassie's mouth fell open. "Topless? You wear nothing on top?"

Dana smiled at her kindly. "That's what topless means."

Cassie hoped she wasn't blushing.

Dana paused in front of a classroom. "I suppose I should make an effort to get into this class on time." She sighed wearily, as if it were more effort than she cared to make. "Maybe we can sit together at lunch."

"Sure," Cassie said. "Uh, I guess I better run if I'm going to get to my class. So, uh, I'll see you in the cafeteria."

She left Dana and practically floated down the hall. She couldn't believe Dana wanted to sit with her! Cassie was almost as excited as she'd be if the best-looking boy at school had asked her! She couldn't wait to tell Barbie and the others.

The second she got out of third-period class, she headed directly for the cafeteria. She wanted to get there before Dana so she could tell Barbie to save another seat. She was so caught up in her thoughts, she practically jumped when someone tapped her shoulder.

"Hey, what's the rush?"

Quickly, she rearranged her startled features. "Oh, hi, Gary." She remembered to toss her head so her hair would bob around her shoulders.

"I didn't get a chance to talk to you in homeroom," he said.

He really did have a cute smile. Funny, she hadn't even noticed him today in homeroom. She must have been too busy looking at Dana.

"What's up?" Cassie asked brightly.

"I was just wondering if you might want to sit together at lunch."

Cassie bit her lower lip. It was already four weeks into the term and she didn't have a boyfriend. But there was Dana . . . well, playing hard to get was never a bad idea.

She smiled regretfully. "I've got plans for lunch. I'm really sorry."

Gary didn't seem particularly torn up. "Well, maybe the cafeteria isn't such a great place to talk anyway. How about tomorrow after school? We could go get ice cream or something."

Cassie cocked her head thoughtfully. "Tomorrow after school? Yes, I think I'm free."

"Great! I'll meet you by the side exit."

Feeling very pleased with herself, Cassie hurried to the cafeteria. Gary might not be the best-looking guy in school or the greatest athlete, but he was definitely acceptable.

Luckily, the food line in the cafeteria wasn't too long. She had just come out with her tray when she saw Dana standing there. She wasn't carrying a tray; instead, she had a small bag with some fancy-looking writing on it. Briefly, Cassie wondered if she should tell Dana that no one at Cedar Park brown-bagged it. But a girl like Dana could probably get away with doing anything she wanted to do.

Dana wasn't looking at Cassie, and Cassie approached her a little nervously. Did she remember their plans?

"Hi," she said tentatively.

Dana acknowledged her with a slight smile and looked at Cassie's tray. "Do they really expect anyone to eat that garbage?"

Cassie hadn't even noticed what was on her tray. Actually, it wasn't all that bad today—fried chicken, green beans, and something brown that was probably pudding.

"I guess they figure we'll be hungry enough to eat anything." She looked around the room, and spotted Barbie and the others. "We're sitting over there."

Dana glanced in that direction. Then she turned back to Cassie. "Couldn't we just eat together, alone?"

"Well, sure, if you want," Cassie replied. Maybe she was shy, like Daphne had suggested. They headed toward a table with empty room at one end. As she passed Barbie, Cassie turned, made a helpless expression and mouthed "Later."

"My sister Lydia always complains about the cafeteria food," Cassie said as they sat down across from each other. "She wants to start a whole campaign to get the school to give us better food."

"Really." Dana didn't look very interested. "Why doesn't she just bring her own lunch?"

As she spoke, she took some little containers out of her bag and opened them.

"What's that?"

"Just a little pâté and a slice of brie."

Cassie figured the brie must be the yellow, runny-looking cheese. It didn't look very appetizing, but Dana spread it on a cracker, took a bite and murmured, "Yum. Want some?"

"No thanks," Cassie said, and decided she'd better offer some explanation other than the fact that it looked gross. "I'm on a diet."

Dana looked at her approvingly. "I'm glad to hear someone around here is conscious of their figure. I've never seen so many chubby girls. And their clothes! Everyone looks so dowdy."

"Really? Do you think Julie and Nancy look dowdy?" Privately, Cassie had always considered them the best-dressed girls in the eighth grade.

Dana dismissed them with a wave of her hand. "They're preppy. In France, nobody would be caught dead dressing like that. Even in Chicago, it's a dead look."

Cassie looked down at her own long-sleeved shirt dress. Was it preppy?

Dana read her expression. "You know, all it takes is a little flair to turn an ordinary look into a fabulous one. All you need with that dress is a small silk scarf around your neck."

Cassie considered this. "Would a cotton one do?"

Dana laughed as if Cassie had said something funny. Then she looked around the cafeteria, and her expression changed. "This place . . . it's such a drag after Paris."

"Were you there with your parents?"

"Just for a little while. Then my father had meetings in Rome and Amsterdam, and my mother was doing a fashion layout in Venice. They sent me and our house-keeper down to the Riviera."

It all sounded so incredibly glamorous. Cassie was awed and dumbstruck. How could she possibly tell Dana about her summer? There was nothing very glamorous about hanging out at the community center pool.

There was so much she wanted to know about Dana, but she didn't want to gush. "How do you like your new home?" she ventured.

Dana shrugged. "It's all right. I have a bigger room than I had in the apartment in Chicago. And there's the swimming pool and tennis court, but they won't be any good till next summer."

Swimming pools and tennis courts. Cassie's head was spinning.

"Hi!" Nancy Ellison was walking past them.

"Hi," Cassie responded, and Dana nodded. Then, when Nancy's back was to them, Dana rolled her eyes and made a face. Cassie couldn't help giggling. She had never seen anyone make a face at a Deb before. It was kind of exhilarating.

She remembered that Dana was in her Spanish class. "That homework yesterday was awful, wasn't it? It took me ages to do that stupid translation."

Dana looked at her blankly. "What homework?"

"For Spanish. You're in my class."

"Oh, right. I didn't do the homework."

Cassie's eyebrows went up. "I better warn you, Senorita Del Sordo really checks that stuff. She's pretty evil when it comes to homework."

Dana smiled. "I'll just pull that jet lag bit on her, like I did in homeroom."

"Hey, Cass!" Cassie saw Lydia hurrying toward her. "Look, tell Mom I might be late today, okay? I've got a Student Council Committee meeting."

"Okay. Oh, Lydia, this is Dana Cunningham. This is my sister Lydia."

Lydia gave her a pleasant "hi," which Dana echoed, but Cassie couldn't help wincing as she noticed Dana taking in Lydia's getup. Lydia was wearing baggy olive green army pants with a very obvious paint stain on one knee. Her purple vest clashed dramatically, and the red bandanna tied around her forehead didn't help the picture.

"Are you the one who came from France?" Lydia asked.

"I spent the summer there," Dana replied. "Actually, I'm from Chicago." She sounded a little bored, as if she'd had to say it a million times, and her eyes wandered. Suddenly, she giggled. "What's that over there—the nerd convention?"

Cassie looked and saw three guys at the next table, huddled over a computer printout. Their hair was unfashionably short, and they all wore glasses.

"For your information," Lydia said, "one of those guys is Bob Howard, who only happens to be a genius. And a friend of mine."

Dana looked amused. "Well, *excuse* me."

Cassie's eyes darted nervously back and forth between them. "I'll tell Mom you'll be late," she said quickly.

"Thanks." Lydia turned to Dana. "Nice meeting you." Her voice was polite, but icy.

"Same here."

Lydia took off, and Cassie turned to Dana apologetically. "My sister loses her temper pretty easily. She's got very strong opinions."

"I can see that. She's a little weird, isn't she?"

Cassie paused. Sometimes she did think Lydia was pretty weird. But for some reason, she felt a little funny admitting that to Dana. "She's . . . unusual, I guess. We're very different," she added hastily.

"Oh, I can see that," Dana assured her. "You don't seem weird at all."

Cassie shifted in her seat uncomfortably. She wasn't sure how to respond to that. After all, it wasn't exactly a compliment.

Dana cocked her head to one side. "In fact, I think we could be friends."

Cassie fumbled for words. "Uh, yeah . . . great."

Dana rose, and Cassie followed, lifting her barely touched tray.

"I want to go fix my face before class. How about you?"

"Oh, absolutely." She picked up Dana's crumpled bag from the table and put it on her tray, then hurried over to stack the dirty tray on the rack, and returned.

Dana smiled at her. "Thanks. Ready?"

"Sure."

And, feeling like a seal of approval was stamped firmly on her face, Cassie walked out of the cafeteria with her new friend.

4

BARBIE WAS WAITING for her on the front steps after school. Her best friend looked just a little bit peeved.

"What happened at lunch? How come you guys didn't sit with us?"

"Dana said she wanted to sit alone with me."

"How come?"

"I don't know for sure," Cassie said. "I mean, it wasn't like she told me any secrets or anything. Maybe she's just a little shy." Privately, she didn't think Dana was shy at all, but she couldn't think of any other reason why she would be reluctant to meet other kids.

"I'm dying to meet her. Is she really neat?" But before Cassie could respond, Barbie added, "Look—here comes the limo."

The big car pulled up to the front of the school, and

once again Dana emerged through the school doors and started down the steps. She saw Cassie and waved. As Cassie and Barbie watched, she spoke briefly to the chauffeur, then ran back up the steps to where they were standing.

"Want to go to the mall?" she asked. "I've got to see if there are any decent shops here."

Cassie looked at Barbie, who was smiling uneasily. Did the invitation include her?

"Dana, this is my friend, Barbie Lane. Barbie, this is Dana Cunningham."

Dana gave her a brief glance. "Hi." Then she turned back to Cassie. "My driver will take us there, and he'll drop you off at home after."

It was obvious that Barbie wasn't being included. Cassie felt a little funny. It wasn't as if she and Barbie had any particular plans, but they did usually go home from school together. On the other hand, Barbie would probably understand. After all, how many opportunities did a person get to ride in a limousine? She could see the kids hanging around the steps ogling the car. She wanted them to see her getting into it.

She glanced at Barbie, who gave a little shrug and stepped back. She understands, Cassie assured herself. "Okay. Uh, I'll call you later, Barbie."

She ran down the steps after Dana. As the uniformed man opened the door for her, she glanced back to see if Barbie was looking impressed. She wished she hadn't. Barbie didn't look impressed at all. If anything, she looked hurt.

But she pushed Barbie's expression from her thoughts as she slid into the back seat next to Dana. It was an amazing car. The seats were real leather, soft and luxurious. There was so much room, Cassie could have stuck her legs straight out in front and not even touched the panel that separated the back of the car from the front. And next to the door, there was a telephone.

"What's that?" Cassie asked, pointing to what looked like a cabinet built into the panel.

"It's a bar." Dana pushed it open, and Cassie saw rows of bottles and glasses. "Want a Coke?"

"Oh, no thanks." Cassie just knew she'd end up totally humiliating herself by spilling it all over the car.

As they pulled away from the school, Dana leaned back into her seat and groaned. "I really hate this place."

Startled, Cassie stared at her. "Why?"

"It's boring," Dana stated flatly.

Cassie considered this. "I guess it would seem that way after Chicago."

Dana uttered a short laugh. "Not to mention New York and London and Rome."

"You've been to all those places?"

"Sure. You've been to New York, haven't you?"

Cassie squirmed a bit. "Well, no, not exactly." What would Dana think of her if she knew she'd never been out of the state of Illinois? Well, there was that time the whole family had gone camping in Wisconsin. But she had a feeling that wouldn't impress Dana.

Dana was silent for a moment. "It's not just that there's nothing to do," she said finally. "It's the people. They're so dull. No one has any style."

Cassie hoped Dana wasn't including her in that description. Self-consciously, she touched her hair, and wondered if she could get her mother to take her into Chicago for a really fashionable cut.

Dana noticed the gesture and smiled. "Of course, I don't mean you. I think maybe you're different."

Cassie perked up. "How do you mean *different*?"

Dana examined her thoughtfully. "I've got this feeling you're not happy with . . . this." She looked out the window at the typical suburban street. "I'll bet you're the type who wants more."

Boy, was she a mind reader! Of course Cassie wanted more. Like an English Mist raincoat, and a great haircut, and clothes that weren't on sale.

"But there *are* some neat kids at Cedar Park," she told Dana. She felt like she had to point out some of the positive things in her school. "Like my friend Barbie. I think you'd like her. And Alison, in our homeroom. Maybe you can join the Pep Club, too."

Dana didn't look particularly enthralled with that idea.

"And there are some cute guys, too," Cassie continued.

Dana's expression made her opinion of that statement very clear. "*I* haven't noticed any. In fact, I haven't seen one boy who I consider even remotely interesting."

"Have you met Gary Stein?"

"Who's he?"

"He's in our homeroom and in our Spanish class. He's got sort of reddish-blond hair, and he always wears a blue windbreaker."

"Oh yeah, I think I know who you mean. What about him?"

Cassie tried to sound nonchalant. "Oh, I think maybe he likes me."

Dana gave her an amused look. "Oh, come on, Cassie—surely you can do better than that." A faraway look came into her eyes. "You would have adored Christophe."

"Who's Christophe?"

"This boy I went out with in France. He was eighteen."

"Eighteen!" Cassie was definitely impressed.

"Of course, he thought I was at least sixteen. He sent me roses, practically every day. And he'd take me out to dinner at the most fabulous restaurants. Then we'd go to a disco and dance all night."

"Your parents let you stay out all night?"

Dana laughed. "Oh, they were hardly ever around. They didn't even know about Christophe. Of course, there was the housekeeper, who was supposed to keep her eye on me. But she was easy to sneak around. She never paid much attention to what I did."

"Lucky you," Cassie said enviously. "Someone's always paying attention to everything I do."

The car had pulled into the mall and come to a stop at the entrance. "You can pick us up in an hour, Charles," Dana instructed the driver.

"Uh, thanks for the ride," Cassie mumbled to him as she got out.

Dana gave her another of her amused looks. "You don't have to thank chauffeurs, Cassie."

Cassie made a mental note to remember that as she and Dana entered the main level of the mall. The first store Dana noticed was a jeweler's. "I need a gold chain," she said. "Let's go in here."

Cassie had never been in that particular store. There were real jewels in the window, engagement rings and things like that, not the kind of stuff she and her friends could ever afford. But Dana breezed in like she owned the place.

"May I help you?" a salesman behind a counter asked.

"I'd like to see some gold chains," Dana said, making it sound more like an order than a request.

"Certainly." The man reached under a counter and brought out a velvet tray on which lay various styles of gold chains.

"Oooh," Cassie said, pointing to one with an unusual squiggly shape. "I like that one."

Dana's expression was unreadable. She lifted one chain, held it in her hand for a moment as if she were weighing it, then put it back. She picked up another, held it against her neckline, and looked at herself in a little mirror resting on the counter. Then she frowned. "Is this fourteen-carat gold?"

"Yes, it is," the man replied.

Dana whipped it off her neck and replaced it quickly. "I never wear anything less than twenty-two–carat gold." With that, she turned to Cassie and said, "This is junk. Let's get out of here."

Cassie turned beet red. How could Dana be so rude? What would the salesman think of them? But by the time she got out of the store, she felt differently. After all, her father always said they should stand up for what they believed in. And her mother was always telling them to be assertive. Dana was definitely assertive.

As they strolled through the mall, Cassie spotted some girls from the Pep Club in front of the record store.

She was about to suggest they go over and say hello, when she realized Dana was already looking at them.

"Those girls are from school, aren't they?"

"Yeah, they're all in the Pep Club. Want to meet them?"

"Not particularly. I hate the way girls travel in packs like that. It's so juvenile. I'd rather just make one good friend and have a real relationship."

Was Dana saying *she'd* be that one good friend? Cassie couldn't believe her good fortune. Of all the girls in the eighth grade at Cedar Park Junior High—many of whom were much better dressed than she—Dana liked her!

"There's a sale at Mirage Juniors," she said, indicating a store.

"I never buy anything on sale," Dana stated. "If it's on sale, that means no one wanted it when it was full price."

Cassie had never thought of it that way. It made sense, though. They walked past the girls in front of the record store. Cassie waved at them, and they waved back. Even from a distance she could see their admiring glances as she strolled with this fascinating new girl.

"Have you got any brothers or sisters?" she asked Dana.

"No, how about you?"

"Well, you met my older sister, Lydia. . . ." She didn't look at Dana as she said that—she'd just as soon not see her reaction to that unpleasant encounter. "And I've got two younger sisters. Daphne's in the seventh grade and Phoebe's still in elementary school."

"There are four of you? You must have a huge house."

"Not compared to yours. It seems pretty crowded sometimes." She grinned. "Luckily, I'm the second oldest, so I don't have to take much in the way of hand-me-downs."

"Hand-me-downs?" Dana sounded as if she didn't know what the word meant.

"Let's look in here," Cassie said hastily. She led Dana into Connections, one of the most popular clothing stores.

"Oh, look," Dana said excitedly, "long dresses!" She went over to a section Cassie had hardly ever explored. It was where the Debs shopped for coming-out dresses and the high school girls went to look for prom gowns.

"What do you think of this?" Dana lifted a dress off the rack and held it in front of her. It was bright red, with hundreds of sequins decorating the top.

"It's great," Cassie said. "But where could you wear something like that?"

"Oh, parties, and nightclubs. . . . C'mon, let's try some of these on." Dana began poking through the racks, pulling out gown after gown.

Well, Cassie thought, it wouldn't hurt just to see how they looked on her. She pulled out a slinky, off-the-shoulder blue silk.

"Do you girls need any help?" A saleswoman was standing there, smiling pleasantly.

"We just want to try some of these on," Cassie said. "Is that okay?"

"Of course," the woman said, but she was looking at

Cassie skeptically. "Maybe these are a bit too old for you, dear. Why don't I show you—"

"We're perfectly capable of selecting our own clothes," Dana interrupted sharply.

The saleswoman raised an eyebrow. "Certainly. . . . As soon as you've made your selections, I'll show you to a dressing room."

Quickly, Cassie grabbed another dress, a lavender one with large puffy sleeves. Dana must have had five or six in her arms when she finally nodded to the saleswoman.

"This way," the woman said, leading them to a dressing room.

Once they were alone, Cassie finally had a chance to look at a price tag. She gasped. "Dana, this one's $275!"

"Yeah, they're really cheap. I guess living in hicksville has some compensations."

If Dana thought these dresses were cheap, she must be even richer than Cassie had imagined. She undressed, and gingerly put on the slinky dress. She'd never even tried on anything this expensive. "How's this?"

"Not bad," Dana said. "Here, zip me up."

Dana looked fabulous—like a movie star. Cassie examined herself in a mirror. "I look silly," she moaned. "Like a kid dressing in her mother's clothes."

"Maybe if you got your hair cut," Dana suggested, lifting Cassie's hair off her shoulders. She definitely looked older that way.

Dana struck a pose before the mirror. "Dah-ling, bring me my mink."

Cassie giggled. She slipped out of the slinky dress and put on the lavender one.

"That looks like something Princess Di would wear," Dana said as she pulled another gown over her hips.

Cassie imitated an English accent. "I cahn't find my crown! What a bloody drag!"

Now Dana started giggling. As they tried on each dress, they made up stories and acted out roles. By the time they were through, they were practically in hysterics.

"What am I going to wear to the ball?" Cassie wailed dramatically. Dresses lay strewn all over the floor.

"Absolutely nothing will do!" Dana replied. She put on her skirt and sweater. Cassie was just buttoning her own dress when the saleswoman poked her head in.

"How are you girls doing . . ." Her voice trailed off as she took in the mess on the floor.

Dana looked at her sternly. "We're doing just fine. Except for the fact that there's nothing in this store worth buying." With that, she pushed past the woman and walked out of the dressing room.

Cassie frantically buttoned the last button and grabbed her purse. "Sorry," she murmured to the woman, who was gazing in dismay at the crumpled heap of dresses.

She followed Dana out of the store. When they looked at each other, they burst into giggles again.

"Let's go in there," Dana suggested, pointing to Dominique's, a store across the mall. It was an exclusive designer boutique, another store Cassie had never bothered to go in.

The atmosphere in Dominique's was different from Connections—quieter, more refined. Cassie and Dana wandered down the aisles, where well-dressed women conferred quietly with elegant saleswomen.

"Those are the kind of scarves I was telling you about," Dana said. She walked over to a display where beautiful, multicolored silk scarves were draped gracefully. She looked at Cassie's dress and scrutinized the display. Then she selected a scarf in shades of yellow and rust. "This would be perfect with what you're wearing." She tied the scarf around Cassie's neck. "Now look."

Cassie gazed into the mirror. Dana was right—the scarf was perfect. It made her simple, ordinary shirtdress look sophisticated, stylish. Then she caught sight of a discreet price tag hanging from another scarf in the display. Forty dollars.

Reluctantly, Cassie pulled off the scarf. "It's terrific," she said, and decided she might as well be honest. After all, Dana was going to have to know eventually that Cassie didn't have the kind of money she had. "But I just can't afford it. Not right now." Or ever, she told herself silently. She handed the scarf to Dana.

Dana's expression was a combination of curiosity and sympathy. Cassie made a point of looking at her watch. "Oh my gosh, it's after five! Didn't you tell the driver to meet us at four-thirty?"

Dana shrugged. "He can wait. That's what chauffeurs do."

"Well, I've got to get home," Cassie said. "I think it's my night to set the table." Dana had probably never set a table in her life. "You probably have to get home, too."

Dana just shrugged. "I can go home anytime I want." But she replaced the scarf on the display, and the girls headed toward the door.

They had just gotten back out into the mall when Dana stopped suddenly. "I think I left something in there. You wait here—I'll be right back."

She ran back into the store. Cassie stood there, looking at her watch and trying to remember if it was her set-the-table night. If it was, she might be in trouble.

It was a full ten minutes before Dana came out, looking a little breathless. "Let's go."

What had she forgotten? Cassie wondered. But Dana had a determined expression on her face, so Cassie just followed her out of the mall entrance to where the limousine was waiting.

As they rode away from the mall, Dana seemed to relax. She smiled brightly at Cassie. "I've got something for you."

She reached into her purse and drew out the yellow-and-rust scarf. "Here."

Cassie gasped. "Dana! You bought this for me?"

"It's just so perfect with that dress. You have to have it."

Cassie fingered the scarf. It felt so soft, so luxurious, so positively elegant. . . . She eyed it longingly, then handed it back to Dana. "I can't take this, Dana. It's too expensive."

Dana looked stricken. "Cassie! I got it for you!"

Cassie felt torn. What would her mother say about accepting a gift like that? She knew perfectly well what her mother would say. On the other hand, her mother didn't have to know . . . and Dana would be hurt if she didn't take it. . . .

She took the scarf back and Dana beamed at her.

"I don't know what to say. I mean, thank you, and—"

Dana brushed her comments aside. "Listen, you're my first real friend here, and I wanted you to have something special. It's no big deal."

Cassie started to tie the scarf around her neck, and then remembered she was going home. She folded it neatly and put it into her purse. "I want to save it for something special," she told Dana.

"By the way, where do you live?" Dana asked.

Cassie told her, and Dana pushed back the glass part of the partition separating the back from the front. "Two thirty-eight Maple, Charles."

Cassie hoped somebody at home would be looking when the limo pulled up. She was in luck—Phoebe was outside. She was in a sweatsuit, on the front lawn.

Cassie was glad someone would see her, but Phoebe looked really dippy. She was running forward, bending over, doing a half-somersault, and then falling over.

"Who's that? Dana asked.

"It's Fee, my youngest sister." She tried to read Dana's expression as she took in the two-story white house that needed a coat of paint.

But Dana only said, "See you in homeroom."

"Right. And listen, Dana, thank you for the scarf—"

But Dana dismissed that as if it were nothing more than a candy bar. "It's nothing. See you tomorrow."

Cassie realized the chauffeur had opened the door and was waiting for her to get out. "Yeah, see you."

She got out, noting with pleasure that Phoebe had stopped in the middle of another somersault attempt and was staring at the car.

The limo pulled away, and, with as much composure as she could muster, Cassie walked toward the house.

"Hey!" Phoebe yelled. "What were you doing in that car?"

"It belongs to a friend of mine," Cassie said haughtily. "Good grief, Fee, you act like you've never seen a limousine before."

Phoebe followed her into the house. "Whose was it? Boy, they must be rich."

Cassie looked at her. "Really, Fee, it's so tacky to talk about money."

Lydia came storming out of the kitchen. "Thanks a lot, Cassie," she said, sarcasm dripping from her voice.

"What did I do?"

"You were supposed to tell Mom I'd be late. It was my day for setting the table, and she was furious at me."

"Well, that's not my problem," Cassie snapped.

Lydia just gave her a look, then went upstairs.

"Cassie, is that you?" her mother's voice came from the kitchen. "Would you give me a hand in here?"

"Sure, Mom, just a second."

Cassie ran up to her room. Lydia was putting a record on their stereo, and she looked up long enough to give Casssie a glare.

"Look, I'm sorry," Cassie said. "But Dana asked me to go to the mall with her, and I forgot."

"Okay, okay," Lydia muttered. "I guess I shouldn't blame you. I forgot it was my turn."

Cassie remembered something. "Did you notice whose turn it is tomorrow?"

"Daphne's."

Well, at least she was safe for her date with Gary. Funny—she had almost forgotten all about that.

Turning away from Lydia, she extracted the silk scarf from her purse and shoved it into a drawer. Somehow she'd manage to sneak it in and out of the house without her mother—or Lydia—seeing it.

"Are you getting to be good friends with that Dana?" Lydia asked.

Cassie didn't like the way she said *that Dana*. "Yeah. Why?"

Lydia made a face. "I thought she was kind of snotty."

Cassie sighed. "Oh, Lydia, she's not a snot at all. For your information, she's very nice. And lots of fun. And *generous*." With that, she turned and left the room.

5

CASSIE STOOD in the cafeteria line and self-consciously adjusted her scarf. She'd slipped it out of the house that morning in her pocketbook and tied it on in the restroom at school. She still ran the risk of running into one of her sisters and having them ask where she got it—but she could always say she borrowed it from someone in homeroom. That's what she had told Barbie. Of course, Barbie had wanted to know who she'd borrowed it from, but Cassie had managed to change the subject.

She couldn't help wondering if the scarf was worth all this aggravation. But it was gorgeous, it matched her blouse perfectly, and she'd already had three compliments that morning. One was from Barbie, which didn't really count—best friends could always be counted on for compliments. But one of the Debs had stopped her in the hall and admired it, adding that she had the exact same scarf in different colors.

And Gary Stein had noticed it too, sort of. Actually, he hadn't really mentioned the scarf, but he'd said something like "You look really great today," and Cassie had known it was the scarf. Maybe he'd thought she'd dressed up especially for him, for their date that afternoon.

When she finally came out of the line with her tray, she saw Dana waiting for her. As they automatically headed toward an empty table, Cassie said, "Listen, I told Barbie and Alison to sit with us today, okay?"

A shadow crossed Dana's face. "Why?"

Why was she being so weird about meeting other kids? "I don't know, I just thought you'd like them. They're really neat, I promise. Barbie's my best friend."

The shadow darkened, and Dana didn't say anything. She just stared at her unopened lunch bag while Cassie nervously began to pick at her food. What was bugging Dana?

The silence was getting on her nerves. Cassie studied her fingernails and searched for a new conversation starter.

"I hate when my nail polish is chipped. I was up so late last night with that stupid Spanish homework, I couldn't do my nails. Did you get that translation done?"

Dana's expression changed dramatically. Her eyebrows shot up, she gave a little gasp, and her hand flew to her mouth. "I left it at home! What am I going to do?"

Cassie appreciated her dismay. Senorita Del Sordo hadn't been too happy with Dana's jet lag story yesterday. Cassie strongly suspected she wouldn't buy this excuse either.

"Can't you call home and have the chauffeur bring it?"

Dana stared at her for a second. Then she said, "He can't. I mean, he's not there. He's taking the house-keeper grocery shopping."

"Do you have a study hall before class? Maybe you could do some of it then."

Dana shook her head. "There's not enough time." Then she brightened. "Couldn't I just copy yours?"

Cassie bit her lip. She didn't know what to say.

"Oh, please, Cassie," Dana continued plaintively. "I'd change some of the words so Senorita What's-her-face wouldn't know. And I'd be eternally grateful." Her eyes were pleading.

Cassie fingered her scarf. Copying homework . . . well, it wasn't exactly like cheating. After all, Dana *had* done the work.

She saw Barbie and Alison approaching the table. "All right," she said quickly, "but don't tell anyone, okay? We'll get it out of my locker after lunch."

Dana rewarded her with a huge smile, and Cassie's uneasiness faded. "Hi," she called brightly to Barbie and Alison. "You guys know Dana, right?"

"Hi, Dana," the girls chorused.

Dana allowed them a small smile as the girls sat down. Then she concentrated on unwrapping her lunch.

From the bag, she pulled out a small carton. Inside, Cassie could see what looked like little mounds of rice with something on top of each mound.

"What's that?" Cassie asked.

"Sushi. It's raw fish. My chauffeur just delivered it, so it's very fresh."

Cassie wanted to gag, but managed to keep her face from showing it. Barbie wasn't quite as cool—she looked distinctly appalled. And Alison came right out and said, "Gross."

Dana gave them both a withering look and directed her next remark to Cassie exclusively. "Do you want to try it? It's very low in calories."

Even that bit of information didn't make the things any more appealing. Cassie thought rapidly. "Uh, no thanks, I'm allergic to fish."

Dana looked at Cassie's tray. "Isn't that tuna salad?"

Cassie examined the half-eaten mound on her tray. "Oh. Yeah, you're right, I didn't even notice what I was eating. Guess I better not eat any more. I might break out or something."

She could feel Barbie's eyes on her. Barbie knew perfectly well Cassie wasn't allergic to anything. But she wasn't about to admit to Dana that the very idea of raw fish grossed her out, too. After all, it was probably a great gourmet delicacy, and she'd have to acquire a taste for it eventually. But not today. She tried to think of a way to get another conversation going.

"How was your Pep Club Committee meeting yesterday?" she asked Alison.

That got Alison started, and for the next few minutes she regaled the group with the story of how two girls almost came to blows over the choice of refreshments for the next meeting. Dana ate her sushi things daintily and looked bored.

"Darryl asked me to the ninth-grade dance next month," Barbie said when Alison had finished.

"That's neat," Cassie said with enthusiasm. This was something that Dana should find interesting.

Dana looked at Barbie skeptically. "You date a ninth grader?"

Barbie nodded happily. "And he's sooo cute."

Dana seemed amused. "Don't you think junior high boys are awfully immature? I do."

Barbie bristled. "Darryl's no more immature than I am."

Dana raised her eyebrows and smirked.

Now Cassie was getting uncomfortable. She turned to Dana. "Look, we'd better go by my locker now, if we're going to, uh, do that before class."

Dana nodded agreeably and stood up.

"I'll see you after school," Barbie said to Cassie.

Dana shot her a hostile look, then turned to Cassie. "I was going to ask if you'd come home with me this afternoon. I finally got my bedroom fixed up, and I wanted you to see it."

Cassie's eyes widened. A chance to see the Dibbley mansion from the inside! "I'd love to," she exclaimed.

She couldn't miss the exchange of glances between Barbie and Alison. And she had to admit it was definitely rude of Dana to ask Cassie in front of the others without inviting them, too.

But surely Barbie and Alison would do what Cassie was doing if they were in her place. Who could pass up an opportunity to see the inside of a real mansion?

She threw them a helpless look. "I'll talk to you later,"

she said. Alison shrugged. Barbie stared at her plate.

For the rest of the day, Cassie was in a perpetual state of daydreaming, trying to imagine what she'd see in Dana's house. Being friends with her was so exciting— limos, mansions, silk scarves—who knew what might come next? Maybe she'd meet Dana's mother, the fashion model, who just might think Cassie had what it took to be a model herself. Maybe she'd end up going to the Riviera with them. . . .

"Cassie!"

Her head jerked up. The teacher was looking at her grimly.

"The rest of the class is discussing ancient Rome. I don't know where you are, but I'd be immensely pleased if you'd join us."

A couple of kids tittered. Cassie blushed furiously and managed a weak "Sorry."

As soon as the last bell rang, she got up to race out of class. Unfortunately, the teacher stopped her.

"Cassie, could you give Lydia a message? Tell her I've got to have that article she's writing by nine tomorrow morning or we won't be able to get it into this week's issue."

Cassie looked at her blankly. Then she remembered Ms. Hunter was the advisor to the school newspaper. "Sure, I'll tell her," she said hurriedly, and ran out.

She met Dana at the main entrance. The limousine was already there, and this time Cassie sauntered toward it as if she was accustomed to getting into limos.

It took only five minutes to get to Dana's. As the limo traveled up the wide driveway that circled the front of

the house, Cassie marveled at the grounds, the mani-
cured lawn, the formal garden.

"It's a beautiful house," she sighed, although *beautiful*
hardly seemed adequate.

"It's okay," Dana said.

Cassie anxiously checked her reflection in a window.
"I hope your parents like me."

"They're not home," Dana replied. "My father's at a
meeting somewhere—Mexico, I think. And my mother's
shooting a TV commercial in New York."

"Gee, they're hardly ever in town," Cassie commented.
"Do you miss them?"

Dana didn't seem to have heard her. The car stopped
in front of the entrance, the chauffeur opened the door,
and they got out. Like magic, the front door of the
house opened for them, and Cassie got a brief glimpse
of a uniformed woman—a maid, she figured.

Once inside, it took her a moment to adjust to the
dim lighting. She was in a long hallway, as wide as a
real room. Large framed paintings hung on the walls.
It reminded her of the entrance to a museum. An
archway led off to the side, and Cassie followed Dana
through it.

"This is the formal living room."

It was like something out of the movies. Cassie didn't
know anything about furniture, but she suspected these
were real antiques—elaborate, stiff-looking sofas and
chairs that looked like no one ever sat in them, heavily
carved tables, big painted lamps.

Dana didn't give her much time to look around. She
breezed through the room to some heavy-looking dou-

ble doors and pulled them open. "And this is the dining room. It's no big deal—a dining room's a dining room."

Cassie couldn't quite agree with that. She counted sixteen chairs around the huge, dark wood table, and the carved wooden cabinets against the walls seemed to hold enough china to serve the entire population of Cedar Park. It certainly didn't resemble the dining room at home, which wasn't even a separate room— just an extension of the living room. And it was only used for special occasions.

"Do you eat in here every day?"

Dana shook her head. "Only when my parents are home. Usually I eat in my room."

The only time Cassie ever got to eat in her room was when she had the flu.

Dana continued the tour—the east parlor, the west parlor, the library, the breakfast room—and the rooms became a blur, a series of elegant environments, each appearing to be straight out of the pages of a decorating magazine. Cassie had to admit that none of them looked like the kind of room where a person might flop on the floor and play a board game—but then, Dana probably didn't do things like that anyway.

From the breakfast room, they went outside to a terrace. Once again, Cassie could only gasp and sigh in awe. The huge free-form swimming pool and cabana, the tennis court beyond that—the back of the house was like a country club.

"It'll be nice this summer," Dana commented.

In her mind, Cassie saw herself sunbathing here, with Dana and a bunch of other elegant people, instead of at the crowded noisy community pool—and she shivered with delight.

Dana misinterpreted her action. "Yeah, it's cold out here. Let's go up to my room."

Back in the main hallway, a stately looking, gray-haired woman came out of one of the rooms and eyed them curiously.

"Aren't you supposed to be at school?" she asked Dana.

Dana rolled her eyes. "It's four o'clock. School's out."

Cassie waited to be introduced, but Dana said no more. The woman nodded vaguely, and passed them by.

"Who was that?" Cassie whispered.

"Housekeeper," Dana said.

"What does she do?"

Dana laughed shortly. "Not much. But at least she doesn't bug me. I could be gone for days and she probably wouldn't even notice."

"But don't you have to be home at a certain time? Like for dinner?"

Dana led her to a staircase, one of those winding kind Cassie had only seen in movies. "I eat when I feel like eating."

Cassie's head was swimming as she followed Dana upstairs. All that freedom! "And I'll bet you can stay out as late as you want."

"Of course!"

They emerged on a hallway lined with closed doors. Dana headed directly to one of them and flung it open. "Here's my room."

If she gasped one more time, Dana would think she was a hick. But it was the most beautiful bedroom she'd ever seen. The carpet was pale lavender, the kind of light color Cassie's mother would never have because it showed the dirt. Of course, there was no dirt on this carpet; servants probably cleaned it every day. The filmy curtains on the windows were the exact same color. The flowered wallpaper displayed soft, muted purple violets, and the fluffy comforter on the huge canopied bed was in the same pattern. All the furniture—bureaus, vanity table, cabinet—was gleaming white.

Compared to the room Cassie shared with Lydia—well, it was like comparing the White House to a log cabin. It couldn't be done.

Dana sauntered over to the cabinet and opened it with a flourish, not unlike a hostess showing off prizes on a quiz show. Inside was a huge television—color, Cassie assumed—and a stereo system with components she couldn't even identify.

Shaking her head in disbelief, Cassie sat down in a white wicker rocking chair. She noticed a telephone on the night stand by Dana's bed. "Oh, you've got your own extension," she said enviously.

"It's not an extension," Dana corrected her. "It's my own private line. Remind me to give you the number."

"You're so lucky," Cassie moaned. She didn't know any other kids who had their own private phone line.

Dana flopped down on her bed. "Yeah." She didn't sound terribly enthusiastic. But then, she was probably so used to all this it didn't impress her anymore.

"Dana, I know this is going to sound weird, but—"

"But what?"

58

Cassie smiled shyly. "Could I look at your clothes?"

Dana laughed. "Sure."

Cassie went over to the closet and opened the double doors. It was a walk-in closet, and immediately Cassie felt like she was walking into the most chic shop in town. Reverently, she touched the garments, admiring the fine materials, the beautiful colors.

Her eyes were shining when she turned back to Dana. "You are definitely going to be the best-dressed girl at Cedar Park Junior High."

Dana didn't respond. She didn't even look at her. She was just sort of staring into space, at nothing. Her eyes had a funny glaze, and she looked a little sad.

"Dana?"

"Huh?"

Cassie sat down next to her on the bed. "Is something wrong?" She spoke hesitantly. After all, they hadn't really known each other very long.

Dana spoke slowly. "I was just thinking . . . about how I've gone to so many different schools. I was never at any place long enough to make friends. I mean, I've never had anything like a best friend."

For the first time, Cassie felt something besides envy and admiration for Dana. She couldn't imagine life without a best friend. "Didn't you have friends in Chicago?"

"Oh, I was always switching schools."

Cassie wondered why, but she didn't think it would be polite to ask. So she just nodded sympathetically.

"I was wondering. . . ," Dana continued, "could we be best friends?"

Cassie was taken aback. She'd only known Dana for

a few days. Best friends—why, people didn't get to be best friends until they'd been just plain friends for a while. And besides, she already had a best friend. On the other hand, she could probably handle having two. . . .

"I guess so," she said hesitantly.

Dana looked so pleased, Cassie almost felt embarrassed.

"That's super," Dana said. "Oh, Cassie, we can have so much fun! You can come spend the night, and we can go shopping—hey, you know what we could do?"

"What?"

"We can go to Chicago for a weekend! I've got an aunt who lives there, and she's hardly ever in town. We could have her apartment all to ourselves. We'll go to restaurants and discos and do all kinds of neat stuff!"

"Sounds great!" For a moment, Cassie wondered if her parents would even consider letting her go to Chicago for a weekend. And where would she ever get the money for restaurants and discos? But she pushed those thoughts aside. Just listening to Dana's plans was enough for the moment.

And Dana didn't stop with Chicago. She went on, talking about Cassie coming with her to Paris, to Rome. She described the places they'd see and the things they'd do with so much enthusiasm that Cassie felt like she was already there.

She was frolicking on the beach somewhere in the South of France when she became aware of a familiar rumbling in her stomach. She was hungry. She turned to look at the clock on the night table. "Yikes! It's almost six!"

"So what?"

"I have to get home!" Cassie jumped off the bed. She didn't think it was her night for setting the table, but she had this funny feeling there was something she was supposed to do. In any case, dinner was at six.

"Don't worry, the chauffeur will take you," Dana assured her.

But when they went downstairs, they discovered the chauffeur had taken the housekeeper somewhere.

"I'd better go now," Cassie said. "Thanks for having me over."

"You don't have to thank me," Dana replied. "I mean, we're best friends, right?"

Cassie thought about Barbie. How was she going to feel about this? Well, Cassie would just have to come up with a way to make Barbie and Dana be friends, too.

"Right," she said quickly. "I'll see you tomorrow!"

"Call me tonight! Do you have a pencil and paper? I'll give you my number."

Cassie burrowed through her purse. She found a pencil and paper and jotted down the number as Dana recited it.

"Okay, I'll call you later," she said hurriedly. It must be after six by now, she thought—she could be in real trouble.

Sure enough, two of the faces that greeted her when she entered through the back door weren't very happy. Dinner was on the table and everyone was eating. This *would* be a night her father had actually made it home for dinner on time.

"Where have you been?" her mother asked. "Do you realize what time it is?"

"I'm sorry," Cassie said. "I was at Dana's and I guess I lost track of time." It wasn't much of an excuse, and she knew it. Even her father looked more than a little annoyed.

"You had us very worried, young lady! You could have called, you know."

"I said I was sorry!"

She hadn't realized how loud her voice was until she saw her sisters all turn and look at her in surprise.

"I don't think I like that tone of voice," her father said.

Cassie dropped her books on the counter and pulled off her coat. "Okay, okay," she muttered, "I'm sorry about that, too."

Everyone was silent as she sat down and she could see her parents exchanging glances. She thought about Dana, who didn't have anyone watching a clock.

"Give me your plate," Mrs. Gray said quietly.

Cassie handed it to her and her mother placed a slice of meat loaf on it. Phoebe passed her the string beans. For a few moments, there was no conversation.

Daphne broke the silence. "What was Dana's house like?"

Cassie avoided her parents' eyes. "It was beautiful—like a palace." She went into a description of Dana's room, making special note of the television, the private phone—everything Dana had that she didn't have.

"Her stereo makes ours look like a kiddie record player," she told Lydia. "And you wouldn't believe the size of the swimming pool!" She gave an exaggerated sigh. "I think Dana must be the luckiest girl in the world."

She knew her parents were exchanging glances again. Well, good—maybe now they'd realize that other kids actually had all those things she wanted.

She wasn't prepared for her mother's next remark. "Cassie, why don't you invite Dana home for dinner?"

Cassie stared at her. Dana—here? Dana, who was accustomed to elegance and servants and formal dining rooms?

"That's a good idea," her father said. "I'd like to meet this paragon of virtue myself."

"Me, too," Phoebe chimed in. "Hey, if she comes in the limousine, do you think maybe she could take us for a ride around the block in it?"

Cassie glared at her fiercely.

"How about tomorrow night?" her mother asked.

Cassie shifted uneasily in her chair. "I don't know," she murmured, wondering if there was any way she could get out of this. It wasn't as if she was ashamed of her family, but she couldn't quite picture Dana with them.

"Call her tonight and invite her," Mrs. Gray said firmly. "Oh, that reminds me, you had a call earlier. Someone named Gary."

A forkful of beans hung suspended in midair. "Oh, no!" She knew she had forgotten something. Gary! She was supposed to have met him after school! "Can I be excused? I have to call him back right away."

"After dinner," Mr. Gray said pleasantly.

"But Dad—"

"*After dinner*," her parents repeated in unison.

Cassie sighed. Suddenly, her appetite was gone. She had stood Gary up. So much for potential boyfriends. And now she had to invite Dana for dinner.

She stared glumly at her plate. Vaguely, she wondered what Dana was having for dinner tonight. Caviar, maybe, or pheasant.

In any case, Cassie had a pretty strong suspicion it wasn't meat loaf.

6

CASSIE, are you planning to get out of bed today? Or did you forget about a little thing called school?"

Cassie ignored the sarcasm in Lydia's voice and rolled over. "I'm tired," she mumbled. "I'll get up in a minute."

"Yeah, I guess you must be pretty exhausted," Lydia commented. "After all, you were on the phone for three hours last night."

"Oh, shut up," Cassie muttered. For the umpteenth time, she wished she had her own room. And she hadn't been on the phone for three hours. It was more like two. Maybe two-and-a-half.

But they hadn't been the easiest phone calls she'd ever made. And as Lydia grabbed her robe and marched out to the bathroom, Cassie took advantage of the silence to let her mind go back to the evening before. . . .

She'd called Gary first. All through dinner, she had tried to come up with a good story—a sudden toothache, maybe, and an emergency trip to the dentist. But there were no private phones in the Gray house except in her parents' bedroom, and that one was off-limits. And it was just her luck, as she sat in the hallway alcove dialing the number, that her mother would choose that moment to start rummaging in the hall closet.

Oh, *why* couldn't she have her own phone like Dana, she thought miserably as she listened to the ringing sound. Even just a crummy extension. . . .

"Hi, Gary? This is Cassie."

She counted a full three seconds of silence before the voice on the other end came back with a bland "Oh. Hi."

She glanced at the closet. Her mother's back was to her, but there was no way she couldn't hear. She sighed in resignation.

"Uh, Gary, I'm really sorry about this afternoon. Something came up, and, well, I know this sounds awful, but the truth is, I forgot."

Another three seconds passed. "Yeah. Okay."

She glanced up. Her mother was leaving the closet and heading for her bedroom. As soon as the door closed, she lowered her voice, trying very hard to sound intense. "Oh, Gary, I can't tell you how positively awful I feel about this. I mean, I was really looking forward to seeing you. I could just kick myself."

"Yeah?"

Was she imagining it, or did his voice sound a tiny

bit friendlier? She tried to picture him sitting there, phone in hand, a smile growing on his face. Suddenly, he seemed even cuter than he had before.

"Maybe we could get together another time," she said hopefully.

"Maybe."

She sighed. Well, she couldn't blame him for having some pride. If the opposite had happened—if he had stood her up—she probably wouldn't have spoken to him for weeks.

"Well, guess I'll see you at school."

"Yeah," he replied. "See you tomorrow."

She felt tired when she hung up the phone. Apologizing and acting humble could really take it out of a person.

Now she had to call Dana. Dialing the number, she envisioned Dana picking up the phone right next to her bed, her very own private phone in her very own private room—and not sitting out in a hallway where everyone could listen.

"Dana, hi—it's me, Cassie."

"Cassie! I'm so glad you called." Dana's voice was positively delighted.

Cassie was startled. Had anyone ever sounded *that* happy to hear from her? "How come?"

"I'm just sitting around being bored."

Cassie marveled at that. How could anyone be bored with their own phone, television, and stereo?

"But guess what?" Dana continued. "I did my Spanish homework!" She sounded like she deserved a medal.

"Gee, I haven't even started it."

"Well, you can copy mine if you like," Dana offered.

"That's okay," Cassie said quickly. "Listen, my mother wants to know if you'd like to come over for dinner tomorrow. I know it's last minute, and you've probably got other plans—"

Dana didn't let her finish. "I'd love to! I was hoping you'd invite me over."

Cassie couldn't believe it. Dana was actually excited. She began rattling on about how she couldn't wait to see Cassie's house and asking what she should wear. But the more enthusiasm Dana displayed, the more anxious Cassie felt. What would Dana think of this place? What if Fee made one of her typical obnoxious babyish remarks and Daphne acted spacey? What if Lydia started blabbing about conspicuous consumption? And what if her mother served something like meat loaf again?

"Cassie, I'm so glad we're best friends now," Dana said.

"Yeah," Cassie murmured. But how long would that last, she wondered. By the time she hung up, her stomach was in knots. Dana's world was so fabulous. What would she think of Cassie's ordinary, dull, not-anywhere-near-fabulous world?

Something else was bothering her, too. She lifted the receiver and dialed another number.

"Hello, Mrs. Lane, this is Cassie. Could I speak to Barbie, please?"

As she waited for Barbie to come to the phone, she examined her fingernails. She absolutely had to find time to paint them tonight. Dana's nails always looked perfect. But she probably had professional manicures.

"Hello?"

"Hi, Barb—it's me."

Barbie's "hi" was subdued.

"Whatcha doing?"

"Homework."

Cassie closed her eyes. This wasn't going to be easy either. In the brightest tone she could muster, she said, "The most awful thing happened to me today! I was supposed to meet Gary Stein after school today and I completely forgot."

That seemed to pique Barbie's interest. "You're kidding! Cassie, he's cute! How could you forget?"

"Well, you heard Dana ask me over, and I was dying to see her house . . ."

"Oh, yeah." Barbie's voice immediately deflated.

"Barbie, you wouldn't believe it, her place is so fantastic." Cassie had just started to describe the interior when Barbie cut her off.

"That's all you talk about anymore! Dana, Dana, Dana. Geez, you'd think she was your best friend or something! Personally, I think she's a snob."

"Oh, Barbie, you're just saying that because you don't really know her yet. Once you get to know her better—"

"I don't want to know her any better. Look, Cassie, I gotta go."

Cassie sighed. "Okay. See you later."

Poor Barbie, she thought as she replaced the receiver. She was obviously jealous. And there was really no reason to be. Barbie was still her real best friend. And Dana would be Barbie's friend, too . . . eventually. And they'd all hang out at her swimming pool next summer.

Cassie stared at the phone. She was in absolutely no mood to attack her homework yet. She called Alison, who was a little more interested in hearing about Dana's house. Then she called Amy, from the Pep Club. And she would have called half the eighth grade if her mother hadn't stuck her head out the bedroom door and ordered her off the phone. There was still homework to do, hair to wash, nails to polish . . .

And now it was morning.

"Cassie, are you feeling all right?" Her mother was standing in the doorway.

Now that was an idea, Cassie thought. If she was sick, she wouldn't have to face Gary, Dana wouldn't be able to come over for dinner . . . "Maybe not," she said tentatively.

Her mother came into the room and placed a hand on Cassie's forehead. "You don't feel like you have a fever."

Cassie considered doubling over and clutching her stomach. But it really wasn't worth it. She'd have to face her troubles sooner or later.

"Cassie, is something bothering you?"

She examined her mother's face. It was concerned, it was caring—but what would happen if she told her mother exactly what was on her mind? She'd probably get a lecture on values.

"Mom . . ."

"Yes?"

"Uh, what are you going to make for dinner?"

Mrs. Gray looked at her blankly. Then her expression cleared. "I was thinking about lasagna. I've got one in the freezer."

Lasagna. Well, at least it was Italian. And Italy was close to France.

"I guess I'm okay," Cassie said, swinging her legs over to the side of the bed. Her mother's expression was still uncertain.

"Well, get a move on, then." Mrs. Gray left the room as Cassie got out of bed and prepared herself for what she suspected wouldn't be one of her best days.

And it wasn't. In homeroom, she flashed her brightest, most flirtatious smile at Gary, but she didn't get much in return—only a half-hearted semismile. But she tried again a few minutes later when she managed to catch his eye, and she could have sworn the smile was wider. But not by much.

Dana wasn't there. At first, Cassie thought she was just late, as usual, but the period passed, the bell rang, and she still hadn't arrived.

Cassie couldn't help but feel a little hopeful. There was a virus going around school. Not that she wanted Dana to be sick or anything—but maybe just a little cold, a sniffle, something to keep her from coming to Cassie's for dinner.

At lunch, she was actually relieved when Dana wasn't standing there waiting for her. Here was her chance to make amends with Barbie. Tray in hand, she edged through the cafeteria crowds to the table where her best friend was sitting with a couple of other girls.

"Hi," she said brightly as she set her tray down. A chorus of "hi"s greeted her, but Barbie's wasn't one of them. Cassie put her tray on the table, sat down, and directed her attention to Barbie.

"Have you decided what you're going to wear to the ninth-grade dance?"

For a second, Barbie's gaze was stony. Then she

seemed to relent a bit. "I thought maybe that gray skirt I got at Connections. With my white sweater. Except gray and white might look kind of boring."

Cassie leaned forward. "You know what would look perfect with that skirt? My dark pink shirt—you know, the real long one. You could belt it around the hips and it would be fantastic."

Barbie raised her eyebrows and started to smile. But before she could say anything, Alison murmured, "Here comes your new friend."

Cassie looked up and saw Dana hurrying toward them. Oh, good, Cassie thought. Now she'll have to sit with all of us, and we can all start being friends.

But Dana didn't sit down. Instead, she acted like Cassie was the only person at the table.

"Hi! I can't stay—I've got to go to the principal's office and get a late slip."

"Where were you this morning?" Cassie asked.

Dana giggled. "Don't tell, but I went to the beauty parlor to get my hair trimmed. I didn't want your parents to think I was a slob!"

Some slob, Cassie thought. Wait till she gets a good look at Fee.

Barbie turned to Dana. "You better be prepared for detention. I don't think the office is going to accept that excuse."

Dana gave her a withering look that clearly said "It's none of your business." But she grinned at Cassie. "I got the housekeeper to sign a note saying I was at the dentist. Oh, and guess what? My mother called from New York last night."

"That's nice."

"Yeah, she says she's bringing me home a fur. And she was really pleased when I told her about you, and about how we're best friends now. What time should I be at your house tonight?"

Cassie tried to avoid seeing Barbie's face. "We eat around six."

Dana looked startled. "Really? So early? You know, in Europe nobody eats before nine."

Cassie smiled thinly. "I guess we're just very American."

Dana laughed. "Okay, I guess I'll just have to be American, too. See you at six."

As she watched Dana walk toward the exit, Cassie could feel Barbie's expression even before she got up the courage to look at her. When she finally did, there was no mistaking where that sudden chilly feeling was coming from.

"How nice that you've got a new best friend," Barbie said evenly. "You need one." And with that, she got up, lifted her tray, and left the table.

It was altogether not a great day. In Spanish, Cassie tried talking to Gary, but all she got was that same expressionless half-smile. She passed Barbie several times in the hallways, but her former best friend wouldn't even look at her. And walking home, all she could think about was that Dana was coming to dinner. Once Dana saw the differences between them, she'd realize they had nothing in common. And that would be the end of that relationship, too.

Walking into the house didn't improve her mood. She tried to see it through Dana's eyes. The furniture was nice enough, but it certainly didn't compare to

Dana's palace. Pages of last night's newspaper lay on the floor. Fee's ancient denim jacket was draped over the arm of a chair. And instead of paintings, there were those tacky family photographs all over the walls.

Phoebe wandered in, clutching a peanut butter sandwich and leaving a trail of crumbs in her wake.

"Fee!" Cassie wailed. "You're making a mess."

Phoebe shrugged. "I'll clean it up. When's the rich girl coming?"

Cassie groaned. "At six. And *please* don't call her that. Hey, you are going to change your clothes, aren't you?"

Phoebe glanced down at her battered jeans and the T-shirt that showed evidence of several assorted snacks. "I guess I could change my shirt. Would that be enough?"

Cassie wanted to suggest an entirely new ensemble, but decided not to press her luck. "Yeah, I guess so. And look, Fee, be really polite, okay? And don't say anything too stupid."

Phoebe looked offended. "Geez, Cassie, I'm not a baby."

Suddenly, Cassie felt a little funny. "Never mind. Is anyone else home?"

"Daphne's upstairs. What are you going to do, give everyone instructions on how to act around Princess Dana?"

Cassie just made a face and ran upstairs. She stuck her head in Daphne's room.

"Daph? Are you busy?"

"Just starting my homework. Why?"

Cassie turned on her sweetest smile. "I was just

wondering if maybe you could straighten up downstairs. You know, Dana's coming, and I'd do it myself except that I've got to clean up my room."

Her other sisters would have told her to bug off, but Daphne nodded. "Sure, I'll take care of it."

"Thanks," Cassie said gratefully, and started out of the room.

"Cassie," Daphne said, "how come you're so nervous about Dana coming? You never act like this when Barbie or anyone else comes over."

Cassie paused. "I guess it's because Dana's house is so grand, and she's used to elegance and all that."

Daphne's forehead wrinkled. "But if she's your friend, she won't care if your house isn't as fancy as hers. I mean, real friends don't care about things like that."

Cassie looked at her pityingly. Daphne was sweet, there was no question about that. But she was so naive.

She crossed the hall to her own room. What a disaster. On her side, there were clothes all over the floor, and her dressing table was a messy clutter of makeup, curlers, and brushes. Lydia's desk was overflowing with books, notepads, and wadded up pieces of paper.

She was almost through hanging up the clothes when Lydia walked in.

"Hi," her sister said, tossing a stack of books on her bed.

Cassie glanced over her shoulder and frowned. "Are you going to leave those there?" When Lydia didn't come back with one of her usual snappy retorts, Cassie turned to look at her. There was an odd expression on her face.

75

"What's up?"

"Not much," Lydia said, throwing herself down on the bed. She lay there silently, staring at the ceiling.

Cassie gazed at her curiously. For a few moments, she pushed aside her worries about dinner and sat down on the edge of Lydia's bed. "What's the matter?"

Lydia didn't say anything at first. Then she finally let her eyes drift down from the ceiling to face Cassie. "I just saw your friend Dana."

"Oh, yeah? Where?"

"Cannon's Five-and-Dime, down in the village square."

"So?"

Again, Lydia was silent for a few seconds before she spoke. "I saw her stealing a lipstick."

"What?!"

Lydia sat up. "I couldn't believe it either. She didn't see me, but I was right behind her and I could see everything. She picked up a lipstick, looked around to make sure no one was watching, and then slid it into her purse."

Cassie stared at her for a minute. Then she tossed her head. "That's ridiculous. Why would Dana steal a lipstick? She could probably buy the entire store!"

Lydia shrugged. "You got me. But I saw her, Cassie. She was shoplifting. I swear, that's what I saw."

There were a lot of names Cassie had called her sister in the past, but *liar* was never one of them. Yet Dana—stealing? A dumb little lipstick that couldn't cost more than a couple of dollars? It just didn't make any sense.

"There's got to be an explanation," Cassie said. "I know! She just forgot to pay for it, that's all."

Lydia looked at her doubtfully. "Then why did she put it in her purse if she intended to pay for it?"

Cassie shrugged. "How should I know? Maybe she didn't realize what she was doing. Maybe she was thinking about something else."

"Cassie—" Lydia began.

But Cassie wouldn't let her finish. "All I know is, Dana's not a thief. She's got no reason to steal some dinky little lipstick, and that's that. Dana's *rich*, Lydia. She could buy a truckful of lipsticks."

"There's a word for people like that," Lydia said darkly. "*Klepto*-something. People who steal things they don't want or need. *Kleptomaniacs*, that's it."

Cassie could feel her temper rising. "Dana's not any kind of maniac. You just don't like her, that's all."

"Look, you just ought to keep an eye on her, that's all I'm saying."

Cassie's voice rose. "And don't you dare even hint about this at dinner tonight!"

Lydia rolled her eyes. "What do you think I'm going to say? 'Hey, girl, hand over that lipstick or I'm calling the cops'?"

"Lydia!"

"Or maybe I should be more subtle. Like, I could say, 'Oooh, I just love that shade of lipstick. Where did you get it?' "

"Lydia! Knock it off!"

"Okay, okay, I was just kidding. Don't get so upset!" She paused. "All right, maybe there is a perfectly good explanation. Maybe I was wrong." Her voice got even lower. "But I don't think so."

Cassie ignored that last bit. She examined Lydia's outfit. Overalls, turtleneck. . . . Not as bad as it could be, but . . . "Are you going to change your clothes before dinner?" she asked.

"There's nothing wrong with what I've got on," Lydia replied.

Cassie heard the sound of a door downstairs. "I hope that's Mom," she said, and ran out of the room. As she walked downstairs, Lydia's accusation rang in her ears. Firmly, she pushed it aside. It just wasn't logical. And she wouldn't believe it.

Mrs. Gray was pulling groceries out of a shopping bag when Cassie entered the kitchen. "Hi, honey. What time is Dana coming?"

"I told her to be here at six. Are we still having lasagne?"

"I took it out of the freezer this morning. And look what I got for dessert." She pulled a fancy bakery box out of a bag and opened it. It was a beautiful, small, elaborately decorated cake—very elegant. Perfect for Dana.

"Gee, thanks, Mom. We're going to eat in the dining area, right? Not the kitchen."

"Sure, if you like. Would you set the table?"

"Okay." She headed for the cabinet. "Mom, could we use the good china?"

"Oh, Cassie," her mother sighed. "That would mean washing and drying every plate first, and we don't have time."

Cassie looked wistfully at the china, but began pulling the everyday plates out. Another thought occurred to her. "Mom, what do people drink with lasagna?"

"I don't know what other people drink, Cassie, but we'll have what we always have—water, milk, or I could make some iced tea if you like."

"Dana says in Europe everyone drinks wine with their meals. Even the kids."

"Well, we're not in Europe," Mrs. Gray said.

Cassie carried a stack of dishes out to the dining table and came back for more. "Is Daddy going to be home in time for dinner?"

"He said he would."

Cassie paused at the doorway. "Could you ask him if he could try not to tell those really dumb jokes?"

Her mother didn't reply, but she looked at Cassie thoughtfully.

Encouraged, Cassie continued. "And could you tell Daphne to watch her glasses so they don't fall into her plate? That's really gross. And maybe you can tell Fee—"

"Cassie," her mother interrupted, "are you ashamed of your family?"

"Nooo. . . ." Of course she wasn't ashamed of them. They were her family, and she loved them. But there was always room for improvement.

"Then stop acting like it," her mother ordered. "If Dana's your friend, she's not going to care if your father tells jokes or if your sister's glasses fall in her food."

Just what Daphne had said. Cassie couldn't believe her mother was that naive, too—at her age, she should know better.

By five of six, Cassie was totally hyped up. She had changed into some nice pants with a long sweater and had checked each of her sisters to make sure they were at least presentable. The living room was immaculate and the table looked very nice, even with the everyday dishes. At the last minute, her mother had taken out the good crystal and given it a quick rinse. The glasses added a touch of elegance to the table.

"She might be late," Cassie warned everyone. She kind of hoped Dana would be—Mr. Gray hadn't come home yet, and despite his tendency to tell silly jokes, Cassie wanted him there. After all, he *was* editor of the *Cedar Park Journal*, and that had to be at least a little impressive.

But precisely at six, the limousine pulled up in front of the house. Phoebe was watching out the window.

"Wow, I wish I could get a ride in that. How much do you think a car like that costs?"

Cassie groaned. That was exactly the kind of remark she didn't want Dana to hear.

"Daphne, you sit over here, okay? Fee, be *polite*, and don't say anything about her being rich. Lydia—"

"Do we have to curtsy?"

Cassie only had time to stick out her tongue at Lydia before the doorbell rang. "I guess I'll get it."

"I guess you better," her mother said, smiling. "The butler's off tonight."

Phoebe started giggling, and even Cassie had to grin as she went to the door. No butlers, no maids, no housekeepers—just us Grays at home, she thought.

Well, maybe it would be a new experience for Dana, she mused as she opened the door.

"Hi, Dana—come on in."

7

CASSIE TELLS US you spent the summer in France," Mrs. Gray said. "That must have been exciting."

"Oh, I've been there before," Dana replied. "I went to boarding school for a while in Switzerland, and I spent all my holidays in France."

"France . . . that's so romantic," Daphne said dreamily. "I've always wanted to see the Eiffel Tower."

Dana wrinkled her nose. "That's for tourists. Nobody who's anybody does stuff like that." She turned to Mrs. Gray. "I like your pearls."

Mrs. Gray fingered the strand around her neck. "Thank you, Dana."

"They almost look real."

Mrs. Gray smiled thinly.

"How come you left boarding school?" Phoebe asked.

Dana just shrugged in response.

Cassie noticed that Lydia was watching Dana with a curious expression. She held her breath when her older sister opened her mouth.

"How do you like Cedar Park Junior?"

Cassie allowed herself a small sigh of relief. Dana shrugged again.

"It's okay, I guess. I mean, school's school. Of course, this is the first time I've ever been to a *public* school." When she said the word *public* her nose wrinkled, as if she was smelling something nasty. "Normally, I'd be in a private school. But by the time we got back to the States, it was too late for me to enroll in one."

Lydia smiled. "Too bad."

Cassie bristled. What did she mean by that? But Dana didn't seem to notice Lydia's tone. Instead, she turned to Mrs. Gray again. "This is a such a cute house. Like a little dollhouse. But doesn't it get crowded?"

Mrs. Gray's smile looked funny. "We manage."

The phone rang just then. "I'll get it," Lydia said, jumping up.

"That's probably your father saying he'll be late," Mrs. Gray sighed.

"Where is he?" Dana asked.

"He's editor of the *Cedar Park Journal*," Cassie explained, allowing a note of pride in her voice.

Dana looked surprised. "This town has its own newspaper?"

"Sure."

Dana giggled. "How funny. There couldn't be much news in a little town like this. How come he doesn't work for a real newspaper, like in Chicago?"

Cassie was spared having to reply, or having to look at her mother's expression, which she suspected was irritated. Lydia came back, and her expression was more than irritated.

"Cassie, that was Ms. Hunter."

Cassie was puzzled. "My history teacher? What was she calling for?"

"Because you forgot to give me a message yesterday. About an editorial for the *Century*."

Cassie looked at her blankly for a moment. Then her hand flew to her mouth. "I forgot! She said you had to turn in the editorial—"

"By nine this morning," Lydia finished. "Thanks a lot, Cassie. Now it won't be in this week's newspaper." She fixed Cassie with an accusing glare.

"Now, Lydia," their mother said placatingly, "I'm sure Cassie didn't mean to forget."

"I'm sorry," Cassie said meekly.

Dana was watching all this with interest. "What editorial?"

Lydia flopped down on the floor. "It was about conspicuous consumption."

Oh, Lydia, be quiet, Cassie pleaded silently.

But Lydia couldn't hear her thoughts. She continued. "That's when people spend a lot of money on things they don't need."

Dana just stared at her. Before Lydia could say any more, Cassie broke in quickly. "Uh, Daphne, what's going on with that committee you're on?"

Daphne was lost in one of her usual daydreams. When she heard her name, her head jerked up. "What?"

"Aren't you on some Student Council committee?"

"Oh, the Social Action Committee. We're organizing the food drive for Thanksgiving."

"What's a food drive?" Dana asked.

Daphne smiled shyly. "We collect food for the needy, and arrange everything in nice baskets. Then we distribute them to people who are poor or unemployed."

Dana sniffed. "My father says those are people who are just too lazy to get jobs."

Cassie could see her mother's face getting red. But all Mrs. Gray did was rise from her chair and smile evenly. "I'm going to check on dinner."

"I hear a car," Phoebe announced, running to the window. "It's Daddy!"

Thank goodness, Cassie thought. We can eat. And everyone can shut up for a while.

"This is delicious," Mr. Gray announced after the first bite of lasagna.

"Thank you, dear," Mrs. Gray replied.

"You know," Mr. Gray said thoughtfully, "I should learn how to cook. It's not right that you should be working full-time and managing things at home. I know the girls help out, but I think I should be doing more."

Dana was listening to this with interest. "Why don't you just get a maid?"

Mr. Gray laughed. "Why not two or three? Maybe we could get a cook and a chauffeur, too."

Cassie closed her eyes in despair. It almost sounded like he was making fun of Dana. She knew he wasn't—he'd never do anything like that. She sneaked a peek at Dana to see how she was reacting. Happily, she didn't look particularly offended.

Mr. Gray helped himself to more lasagna. "There's supposed to be a good cooking class over at the adult education center. If I could just find the time . . . Maybe when this series is done."

"How's the series coming?" Lydia asked.

"Pretty good," Mr. Gray replied. "We had a lot of response to last week's article. It's upsetting a lot of people, but I think that's a positive sign."

Mrs. Gray agreed. "It's very important that people become more aware of these problems if they're going to do anything to solve them."

Cassie turned to Dana. "My father's newspaper is running a bunch of articles about the problems teenagers have."

Dana looked puzzled. "What kind of problems?"

Mr. Gray smiled at her. "Well, last week we dealt with eating disorders. Later, we'll be publishing articles on teen pregnancy, drug use, suicide . . . the whole sad situation."

Dana made a face. "That's depressing. Who wants to read about things like that?"

"Nobody wants to hear these things," Mr. Gray said. "But these kids need help."

Dana shrugged. "They should just help themselves."

Lydia looked like she was ready to explode. "You know, not everyone's as lucky as you are."

Dana's eyes narrowed. "Well, that's not my problem."

Cassie watched them nervously. "Uh, Dad, what's next week's article about?"

"It's about the signs to watch for that might indicate a kid's in trouble. There are a lot of signals kids give out when they want attention—cutting school, staying out late, shoplifting. . . ."

Without looking, Cassie knew Lydia's eyes were on her. And she was immensely grateful when the phone rang. "I'll get it," she said, jumping up.

She ran into the kitchen and grabbed the phone. "Hello?"

"Uh, could I speak to Cassie please?"

"This is Cassie."

"Hi, this is Gary."

Cassie clutched the phone tightly. "Hi, Gary."

"Um, look, I was thinking. I guess I wasn't too nice about what happened yesterday. I mean, people do forget . . ."

Cassie tried to help him along. "I really was sorry."

"Yeah, me too. Maybe we could try it again."

Cassie grinned happily. Another chance! "I'd like that," she said carefully.

"How about Saturday? We could go to the four o'clock movie at the mall."

"Great," Cassie said. "I'll meet you there."

Going back to the table, she was feeling so pleased that it took her a full moment before she realized her mother was looking at her strangely. When she spoke, her voice had a funny edge to it.

"Cassie, you didn't tell me you and Dana were planning to go to Chicago for a weekend."

Cassie looked at Dana, who was calmly picking at her salad. "Well, it wasn't actually a plan. We were just sort of talking about it."

"Wow, a whole weekend in Chicago," Phoebe exclaimed. "Boy, if I had a whole weekend in Chicago, I'd spend it all at the Museum of Science and Industry. That's the neatest museum in the world."

Dana gazed at her condescendingly. "I think Cassie and I could find better things to do in Chicago than hang around a museum."

Cassie could feel her good spirits drifting away. Dana didn't have to sound so snide. Phoebe was only giving an opinion.

"Have you asked your parents about this?" Mrs. Gray asked Dana.

Dana brushed that aside. "Oh, I don't have to ask them. They wouldn't care."

Daphne looked shocked. "How can your parents not care what you do?"

"That's really none of your business," Dana replied sharply.

Now Cassie was a little shocked. Daphne hadn't meant anything mean.

"Mom, can I get dessert?" Phoebe asked.

Their mother nodded, but her eyes were on Dana, who stood up.

"Would you excuse me for a moment?" she asked politely. Not waiting for an answer, she left the table and headed upstairs.

There was a long silence at the table. Phoebe returned with the fancy cake.

"Where'd Dana go?" she asked.

"Bathroom, I guess," Cassie said.

"Probably wants to put on some lipstick," Lydia added.

Cassie glared at her, expecting to see a smirk. But Lydia wasn't smirking. If anything, she looked a little sad.

8

CASSIE KNEW HER PARENTS were talking about her when she walked into the kitchen late Saturday morning. She knew from the way they stopped talking, exchanged glances, and then, in unison, turned to her and smiled.

Here it comes, she told herself: lecture of the week. She armed herself with a diet soda and joined them at the table.

"We were just talking about you," her mother said.

What a surprise, Cassie thought. Aloud, she asked, "What did I do?"

"It's nothing you've done," her father said. "It's this new friend of yours, Dana."

She should have known. "What's wrong with Dana?"

Her mother seemed to be choosing her words carefully. "You haven't known her very long, have you?"

"A week."

Mrs. Gray's brow puckered. "And yet, you spend so much time with her."

Cassie shrugged. "I like her."

"I can see that," her mother said. "And I'm not telling you to stop liking her. I'm just concerned because I think your friend has some problems, and—"

"Problems?" Cassie shook her head vigorously. "Dana doesn't have any problems. She's got everything. She's got her own room and her own phone and a swimming pool—"

"Having a room and a phone doesn't necessarily make a person happy," her mother said calmly.

"Sure it does!" Cassie said brightly. "At least, it helps!"

Her father rubbed his forehead wearily. "That's what's bothering me. It seems to me that you're picking up the wrong kind of values from her."

Cassie rolled her eyes. "Daddy, I didn't get any values from Dana."

"That's right," Mrs. Gray told her husband. "Cassie had those values long before she met Dana."

"Well, Dana's reinforcing them." He sighed. "It's not just the values, anyway. Listening to Dana the other night at dinner, I couldn't help but feel that she's a very troubled young lady. There's something about her attitude . . ."

"Oh, Daddy, you're just saying that because of your series. Now you think every teenager has problems."

Her mother shook her head. "Cassie, you heard her say her parents don't care what she does. If that's true, then Dana has some real problems. And if it's not true, she couldn't have a very good relationship with them."

89

They just weren't going to let up. "What she meant was that her parents aren't constantly bugging her and criticizing her all the time. Not like some parents I know."

"Cassie!" her mother exclaimed.

But Cassie didn't want to hear any more. She stood up. "You never bug Lydia about her friends! You don't pick on Fee or Daphne that way you pick on me! It's always me who gets hassled!"

Personally, she thought she sounded pretty dramatic. But neither of her parents looked particularly impressed.

"Don't talk nonsense," her mother said.

"Nobody's hassling anyone," her father added. "We're just concerned about your relationship with Dana."

"Are you telling me I can't hang out with her anymore?"

"Of course not," Mrs. Gray said. "I just want you to realize that there may be more to Dana than meets the eye. And I don't want you to get involved in something you can't handle."

Cassie made an exasperated noise. "Is it okay if I go to the mall with her today? I don't *think* she's planning to burn it down."

Her mother nodded, but she still looked disturbed. "Have a good day."

Cassie turned to leave, and then remembered something else. "Oh, I almost forgot. I'm meeting Gary Stein at four to go to the movies. So I might be late for dinner, okay?"

Her mother actually looked interested. "Who's Gary Stein?"

"A guy from school." She knew why her mother seemed pleased—she was just happy Cassie was spending time with someone other than Dana. But all she said was "Have fun," and Cassie left the room before they could come up with any more advice.

She ran upstairs to get her purse. Lydia was on the phone in the alcove. "Hold on," she was saying, and turned to Cassie. "I'm going bowling with Martha Jane. Want to come?"

"No, thanks," Cassie said. "I'm going to the mall with Dana."

Lydia mumbled something.

"What did you say?" Cassie asked sharply.

"I said, don't let her get near any lipsticks."

Cassie didn't even bother to make a face at her. She ran into the room, grabbed her purse and left, practically colliding with Daphne in the hall.

"Where are you going?" Daphne asked.

"To the mall. With Dana."

"Oh."

"Okay, you don't like her either," Cassie snapped. "Well, I don't care." She turned away quickly, but not fast enough to miss Daphne's stricken expression.

She stormed back down the stairs, grabbed her jacket, and ran out of the house. She'd wait for Dana outside.

What was the matter with all of them, anyway? Okay, maybe Dana was a little different. And maybe she showed off sometimes. But they were all acting like Cassie had become buddy-buddy with some wacko!

She tapped her foot impatiently. Dana was late. Cassie was almost ready to go back inside and call her when the limousine pulled up.

"I tried to call you to tell you I'd be late," Dana said as Cassie got in the car, "but the phone was busy."

"Lydia was on it."

Dana's nose wrinkled. "No offense, Cassie, but I think Lydia's pretty weird. How can you stand sharing a room with her?"

Cassie shrugged. "It's not so bad." Funny—she herself frequently used the term *weird* in relation to Lydia. But hearing it from someone outside the family made her feel a little peculiar.

Dana leaned back in her seat and stretched. "Well, it would drive me nuts having all those sisters around. Not to mention parents."

Cassie shifted uncomfortably. "Don't you ever miss having your parents at home?"

"Oh, sometimes—a little. I mean, my mother's very cool. When she's in town, we go out for lunch and then spend all day getting haircuts or manicures or sitting in a sauna at a health club."

"What about your father?"

"He's okay, too. At least they don't bug me."

Something about her tone made Cassie feel defensive. "My parents don't bug me all that much . . . ," she began, and then stopped. What was she saying? She'd just spent a whole morning being bugged!

"Have you talked to your mother again about coming with me to Chicago for a weekend?"

"No, not yet." Cassie sighed. "I don't think they're going to let me go. They'll say I'm too young."

Dana looked at her sympathetically. "Poor Cassie."

For some reason, that made Cassie bristle. Okay,

maybe she didn't have all the freedom Dana had, but "poor Cassie"? She didn't have it *that* bad.

Dana reached over and patted Cassie's shoulder comfortingly. "Why don't you come home with me this afternoon after we finish shopping? We can get some movies from the video store at the mall and watch them on my VCR."

"I can't today," Cassie replied. "I'm meeting Gary Stein at the movie theater at four."

Dana looked at her in disbelief. "Gary Stein? That short boy with all the freckles?"

"He doesn't have that many freckles!"

Dana grimaced. "He looks like he's ten years old. Honestly, Cassie, can't you do better than that?"

Cassie glared at her. "There's nothing wrong with Gary Stein! Personally, I think he's cute." She turned away from Dana and stared out the window. The car was silent. When she finally turned back and looked at Dana, she was startled to see her friend looking like she was on the verge of tears.

"Dana! What's the matter?"

Dana's lower lip trembled as she spoke. "Are you mad at me?" Her voice sounded almost babyish.

For a second, Cassie was at a loss for words. She'd never seen Dana like this. "No, I'm not mad," she said finally.

Dana smiled brightly. "Good. Because you *are* my very best friend, and I couldn't stand it if you were really angry at me."

Cassie eyed her uneasily. This was getting strange. . . .

But by the time the limo pulled up to the mall, Dana

seemed like her old self again. They stopped first at a record store, where Dana bought two albums. Next, they went into a drugstore, and Cassie got a mascara.

That was all she had money for—but Dana had enough for a lot more shopping. Over the next hour, she bought a pair of large hoop earrings, some patterned stockings, and a lace camisole.

They were approaching a shoe store when she announced, "I need some navy blue heels."

Cassie uttered a silent groan. She had never thought in a million years that she'd ever get sick of shopping. But tagging after Dana from store to store and watching her buy practically everything in sight wasn't her idea of a perfect day. She knew part of her mood was due to envy. But as she slumped in her seat while Dana tried on pair after pair of shoes, she had to admit she was feeling something else, too. Bored. When she went shopping with Barbie, neither of them had much money to spend, and half the fun was imagining what they would buy if they *did* have more money.

"These are ugly," Dana said petulantly to the salesman. She pulled off the shoes and practically threw them down. "Don't you have anything more fashionable?"

"This is the latest style," the man said mildly. "Look at the—"

"Don't tell me what to look at!" Dana was practically shrieking. "I know what I want! And this store is too crummy to have it!"

The tone of her voice made the salesman step back.

"Dana, let's go," Cassie said quickly. "I'm getting hungry."

Dana didn't reply, but she began putting her own shoes back on. She rose and headed for the door.

"Let's get something to eat," Cassie suggested outside the store. At least she had enough money for a slice of pizza.

"I want to go to Connections first," Dana said. "We can eat after that."

Cassie wasn't too crazy about the way Dana said it, like she was in charge. And her stomach was rumbling. But she didn't want to insist—Dana was behaving so oddly today.

It was a typical Saturday afternoon in the trendiest shop at the mall. There was a sale going on, so the store was even more crowded than usual. Flustered-looking salespeople were scurrying around assisting customers. Girls snatched clothes off racks, off tables, and sometimes out of each other's hands. Cassie spotted several classmates from Cedar Park Junior and waved.

Dana selected several sweaters, two skirts, and three blouses to try on. "Aren't you going to try anything on?" she asked Cassie.

Cassie hated to admit she didn't have any money. But she also hated trying on something when she knew there wasn't any way she could buy it. "I'm not in the mood."

Dana was, though. Once inside the dressing room, she tried every possible combination of the clothes she'd brought in. Cassie leaned back on the floor and watched.

"That's cute."

Dana examined herself in the mirror. The turquoise blouse and print skirt fit her beautifully. "Yeah, I might get this." She turned and scrutinized herself from every angle. "I think maybe the blouse would look better in a smaller size."

"That one fits fine," Cassie objected. "What size is it?"

Dana checked the tag. "Medium . . . I think I need a Small."

Privately, Cassie thought a Small would be much too snug, but she didn't say anything.

Dana turned to her with a sweet smile. "Would you go out and get me a Small? *Please?*"

Cassie nodded reluctantly and dragged herself up. She was really hungry—and it was already three o'clock. If they were going to get something to eat before she had to go meet Gary, they'd better hurry.

She went out to the rack of blouses and began fumbling through them. They were really pretty, and they were on sale: $29.95, marked down from $42.50. It was a good deal, and Cassie regretted not being able to get one for herself. Dana would probably buy one in each color.

She found another turquoise one, but it was a Large. She pushed blouse after blouse aside, checking the sizes. Finally she located a Small and took it back to the dressing room.

To her surprise, she found Dana had changed back into her own clothes. "Here's the blouse."

"I changed my mind," Dana said hurriedly. "Come on, let's get out of here. I'm hungry."

At last! Cassie grabbed her purse and the girls walked back out through the store toward the exit. Dana reached the door first and pushed it open. Cassie followed. But just as she stepped out, a loud buzzer went off.

Suddenly a woman was standing there. She placed a hand on Cassie's arm. "I'm going to have to ask you to come with me."

Cassie looked at her blankly. "What?"

The woman spoke quietly but firmly. "You know what I'm talking about. Now just come along and don't make a fuss."

Cassie just stared at her in bewilderment. Then she looked at Dana. Her friend's face was pale.

They followed the woman back through the store. Cassie's face was burning as she noticed several girls staring at them. What was going on here? Were they in trouble because Dana had left all those clothes on the dressing room floor?

The woman led them into an office at the back of the store. By now, Dana seemed to have recovered her wits, and she spoke angrily. "I don't know what's going on here, but there's obviously been some sort of mistake. And if you think I'm going to—"

The woman didn't let her finish. "Just open your purse, please."

Dana jerked open her purse and thrust it in front of the woman. "See? Can we go now?"

The woman turned to Cassie. "Now you, please."

This is ridiculous, Cassie thought, but her heart was beating wildly. She opened her pocketbook.

And then she gasped. Lying there on top of her wallet, makeup bag, and assorted junk, was a turquoise blouse.

9

DIDN'T TAKE IT. I didn't take it."

Even in her panic, Cassie knew she sounded like a broken record, but she didn't know what else to say. The two girls were seated, side by side, in the manager's office. Cassie kept looking at Dana, waiting for her to speak up. But Dana just sat there staring straight ahead, stony-faced, saying nothing.

The woman didn't seem to care. She whipped out a pad of paper. "Your name and telephone number, please."

Cassie's voice trembled as she gave the information. With a sinking heart, she watched the woman go to a desk, pick up the telephone, and dial.

"Am I speaking to the mother of Cassandra Gray? This is the security guard at Connections. Your daughter has been apprehended in an attempt to leave the store with an item she did not purchase."

There was a pause. Cassie couldn't even imagine what her mother was saying.

"Yes, you heard me correctly. No, we have not yet called the authorities. Would you please come to the store so that we can discuss this matter."

Mrs. Gray apparently agreed, and the guard hung up the phone. "Stay here," she ordered the girls, and left the office.

Cassie turned to Dana frantically. "I can't believe it! Why did you do that?"

Dana shrugged. "It's okay. They won't arrest you or anything. The worst they'll do is make your parents pay for the blouse."

Cassie stared at her, aghast. She actually sounded like she'd been in this situation before! "But why did you do it? You could buy ten of those blouses!"

Dana just shrugged again. "I felt like it."

Cassie could feel the anger churning inside her. "But you put it in my bag! Why didn't you put it in your own?"

"It wouldn't fit in mine." She actually had the nerve to giggle a little as she said that. "Look, Cassie, it's no big deal, really. Don't make such a fuss."

Cassie could barely speak, she was so furious. No big deal? Don't make a fuss? Dana had just committed a crime! And Cassie was going to be blamed for it!

"It's a big deal to me!" Cassie exclaimed. "And you'd better tell that lady I didn't do it!"

Before Dana could reply, the door opened and the guard returned with the store manager.

"Which one is the perpetrator?" the manager asked the guard. She indicated Cassie, but Cassie turned reproachful eyes on Dana. Dana wouldn't meet them.

"*Dana*," Cassie said urgently.

"Are you aware that shoplifting is a criminal act?" the manager asked.

Cassie felt hot all over. That man was calling her a criminal! She looked at Dana again. When her so-called friend didn't say a word, an awful realization dawned on Cassie. Dana had absolutely no intention of confessing! She was going to let Cassie take all the blame!

Well, Cassie wasn't about to stand for that. She faced the manager squarely.

"I didn't take the blouse. She did!"

The manager rubbed his forehead. "Sure, sure. And she put it in *your* purse. Look, we assume you two were in this together. But *you*—" and he pointed an accusing finger at Cassie, "—you're holding the stolen property."

"But I didn't have anything to do with this!" Cassie wailed. At that moment, her parents walked into the office. Cassie could barely bring herself to look at them.

"Mom, Dad, I didn't do it," she blurted out before they could say anything. "I didn't take that blouse, honest." She raised her eyes to look at them. They didn't seem angry, exactly. If anything, they looked bewildered.

The manager and the guard took them aside to a corner of the room, where they had a whispered conversation. Cassie turned to Dana angrily. She was startled to see Dana's eyes burning with an anger even fiercer than Cassie's.

"I can't believe you told on me," Dana hissed. "Don't ever speak to me again."

Cassie's mouth dropped open. She was just about to tell Dana that that was fine with her when her parents approached.

"Cassie." Her father's voice was soft and calm. "The store isn't going to press charges. We can leave now. Dana, we'll drop you at home."

Cassie got up and followed them out of the store. Flushed with shame, looking neither to the left nor the right, she knew that by Monday it would be all over school: Cassie Gray had been caught shoplifting.

The ride home was silent. When they reached Dana's place, Dana didn't even thank the Grays for the ride. She jumped out of the car and slammed the door.

Cassie took a deep breath and spoke to her parents.

"I didn't do it. I didn't take that blouse. Dana must have put it in my purse when I was out of the dressing room."

Her father spoke over his shoulder. "We believe you, Cassie."

Cassie sighed gratefully. That was a relief. So instead of a lecture on shoplifting, she'd get a lecture on choosing the wrong companions. And for once, she'd have to agree with her parents.

"That girl," her mother said, shaking her head. "I could just strangle her! Shoplifting is bad enough. But putting the blame on an innocent friend—that's disgusting. Cassie, I don't want you hanging around that girl again, is that understood?"

"I won't, I promise," Cassie said fervently. "I can't

believe I was ever friends with her. She's positively evil! I never want to see her again, *never*!"

"I'm very glad to hear that," her mother replied. "And I'm not even going to say 'I told you so.' "

"Maybe she'll rob a bank next," Cassie muttered. "Then they'll have to put her in jail."

"Now, hold on a second," Mr. Gray broke in. "Don't you think you're being a little rough on the poor girl?"

"Poor girl!" Mrs. Gray exclaimed. "David, you're not defending what that wretched child did, are you?"

"No, no, of course not," Mr. Gray said. "But I can't help thinking she's a girl with problems. Maybe we should show her a little compassion."

"You mean, feel sorry for her?" Cassie's voice rose in disbelief. "Dad, she's got everything! She's rich!"

"That's just the point," her father continued. "Obviously, she doesn't *need* to steal. There must be some underlying problem that's making her behave like this."

"You're thinking about those kids you've been writing about," Mrs. Gray murmured.

"Exactly," Mr. Gray replied. "Maybe Dana is one of those kids."

Her mother lapsed into silence, and Cassie pondered this. Dana—a troubled adolescent? No way. Spoiled brat was more like it.

When they arrived home, Phoebe and Daphne were sprawled on the living room floor, playing Scrabble. They stopped when Cassie and their parents walked in, looking up expectantly.

"Are you going to jail?" Phoebe asked.

"Don't be silly, Fee," Daphne said, getting up from the floor. She threw her arms around Cassie. "I know you didn't do anything wrong. It was all a mistake, right?"

"Right." Cassie was touched by her sister's concern. And after she had been so nasty to her that very morning. She sank down on the sofa.

"You had a phone call," Phoebe told her. "Someone named Gary. He sounded kind of angry."

Cassie buried her face in her hands. It was the final straw. "It's all Dana's fault," she cried, and proceeded to call Dana every nasty name she could think of. Her mother sat down beside Cassie and put an arm around her, while her father and sisters gazed at her in silent sympathy.

Her mother handed her a tissue, and as Cassie blew her nose, she thought about what a nice family she had. She heard the back door slam, and a second later Lydia came bursting into the room. "Hi," she called out cheerfully, and then got a glimpse of Cassie's face. "What's going on?"

"You were right about Dana," Cassie said, sniffling. "She *is* a thief."

Lydia's eyes widened, and she turned to their parents. Briefly, Mrs. Gray told her what had happened.

"Wow," Lydia said. "That girl's got real problems."

Cassie looked at her indignantly. "*She's* got problems? You sound just like Dad!" She turned to see if her mother was looking outraged, too.

"Maybe they're right," Mrs. Gray admitted. "Obviously something's very wrong with Dana. Maybe we should be feeling sorry for her."

"Feel sorry for her? I hate her!" Cassie cried out passionately. "I never want to see her again!"

"Honey, you're exhausted and upset," Mrs. Gray said. "Why don't you go upstairs and lie down?"

She *was* tired, and her head hurt. It seemed like every step up the stairs was a major effort. Even so, when the phone rang in the alcove, she automatically picked it up.

"Hello?"

"Cassie, it's Barbie. I just heard what happened at Connections!"

Cassie gasped. "How did you find out so fast?"

"Alison's sister works there. She told Alison and Alison called me right away."

Great—that meant half the eighth grade would know within the next half hour, Cassie thought.

"Oh, Barbie," she said miserably, "it was awful. And no matter what anyone says, I didn't do it. I didn't take that blouse. Dana took it and stuck it in my purse."

"I figured it was probably something like that," Barbie said. "That's what Alison thought, too."

Waves of relief passed over Cassie. At least people didn't think she was a thief. "You know, Barbie, you're a lot smarter than I am," she said humbly. "You saw through her right away, didn't you?"

"Well, I thought she was a little strange."

"So did my parents," Cassie said. "So did Lydia. So did just about everyone except me. Boy, was I stupid."

"We all do stupid things sometimes," Barbie remarked.

"Yeah. But how many people almost get arrested for it?" Cassie put her hand to her head. Her headache was getting fierce. "I'll see you tomorrow, okay?"

She went to her room and lay down. She couldn't

sleep, though. She kept seeing images of herself, gaping and gawking at Dana's clothes, Dana's house, Dana talking about Paris and the Riviera and boys who took her dancing. And then her idol turned out to be a common criminal!

Lydia came into the room and sat on the edge of her bed. Cassie looked at her glumly. "I hope you're not going to say 'I told you so,' even though it's true."

Lydia grinned and shook her head. "It must have been pretty scary in that store."

"No kidding." The memory made Cassie shiver. "It was awful. I didn't know what was going on."

"I wonder why Dana does things like that," Lydia mused.

"I don't know and I don't care," Cassie said promptly. "I just know I'm going to stay away from her from now on."

"Dad says maybe she does it to get attention."

"Maybe," Cassie said, but she was only half-listening. She was wondering if she should call Gary. She wasn't in the mood to talk to anyone right then, but she had to call him sometime. And when she did, she planned to tell him everything. She wanted everyone to know the truth about Dana, and how she had been deceived by that crook. Cassie didn't care if she destroyed Dana's reputation forever—she deserved it.

But what if Gary didn't believe her? Well, it was something else she could blame on Dana—blowing her chance with a really neat guy.

Her headache wasn't going away, and it dawned on her that she hadn't eaten anything all day. "What's for supper?" she asked Lydia.

"Mom and Dad are going out so they said we could order a pizza."

"Great, but I need a cookie or something now. I'm starving."

As she passed the phone in the hall, it rang.

"Hello?"

"Hi, it's me."

Cassie couldn't believe her ears. How could Dana dare call her now?

"Cassie? Are you there?"

Cassie considered hanging up, but Dana would probably call right back. "What do you want?" she asked in a voice as cold as she could make it.

"I just wanted to let you know I've decided to forgive you."

"What?!"

"I'm going to forgive you for telling on me."

"Well, that's just great," Cassie said in the most sarcastic tone she could muster. "I really appreciate it."

"What's the matter with you?" Dana asked.

Cassie felt like exploding. "Are you nuts? You stole that blouse and you tried to blame it on me! And you're going to forgive me? Well, I'm never going to forgive you!"

She slammed the phone down as hard as she could. She stood there, staring at the phone, as her mother came out of the bedroom.

"What's going on? I heard you yelling."

"That was Dana on the phone. She says she forgives me for telling on her. Can you believe that?"

"What did you say?" her mother asked.

"I hung up on her."

Her mother put an arm around her shoulder. "Don't be too hard on her, honey."

Cassie shook her head in bewilderment. "This is unreal. One minute everyone's telling me not to hang around with her. And now you're all saying I should feel sorry for her."

Her mother bent down and kissed her on the forehead. "I know it's hard for you to understand someone like Dana. We'll talk about this later. Right now I've got to run, or your father's going to pass out from starvation."

Cassie was still shaking her head as her mother walked away. Talk about starvation. She reached for the phone. The only thing she could understand right now was a pizza. With everything.

The world looked a lot brighter when it was covered with pepperoni and mushrooms. By the time she started on her second slice, Cassie felt a zillion times better.

"I don't get it," Phoebe said, picking mushrooms off her slice. "Why does Dana steal things if she can afford to buy them?"

"Can we please stop talking about Dana?" Cassie asked plaintively. "I'm sick of hearing her name."

Daphne tried unsuccessfully to muffle a giggle, and Cassie looked at her. "What's so funny?"

Phoebe answered for her. "Because we were just saying this morning that we were sick of hearing you talk about Dana all the time."

Lydia sauntered into the kitchen, looking disgruntled. "Hope you guys saved some for me," she muttered as she sat down.

"What's the matter?" Daphne asked.

Lydia scowled. "I just got off the phone with that idiot George Philips. It's unbelievable that that guy is actually editor of the *Cedar Century*."

Cassie remembered how much Lydia had wanted to be made editor. She never missed an opportunity to complain about George. "What did he do now?"

"I told him I thought we should do a series of articles like Dad's doing in the *Journal*. We could write about the same kind of problems, only ours would deal with the kids at Cedar Park Junior."

"But kids at Cedar Park Junior don't have problems like that," Cassie objected. "Not like the kind Dad's been talking about."

"I'm not so sure about that," Lydia replied. "I wish I could start my own newspaper."

The phone rang, and Daphne got up to answer it.

"Hello? Uh, hang on a minute." Daphne covered the mouthpiece with her hand. "Cassie, it's for you."

Cassie started to get up, and then Daphne added, "It's Dana." Cassie sat back down again.

"Tell her I don't want to talk to her."

Daphne spoke into the phone. "Uh, I'm sorry Dana, but she can't come to the phone right now. But I'll tell her you called."

When she hung up, Cassie frowned at her. "Why did you say that?"

"I didn't want to hurt her feelings," Daphne admitted. "I feel sorry for her."

Cassie groaned. "Not you, too! *Why* does everyone feel sorry for her?"

Daphne looked thoughtful. "When she was here for dinner, I thought she looked sad."

"It must be awful thinking your parents don't care about you," Phoebe added.

Cassie reached for another slice. "That doesn't give her the right to be a shoplifter." She was just about to bite into her slice when she remembered something. She jumped up. "I'll be right back. Don't anyone take my pizza."

She went into her mother's study and got a large brown envelope and a pen. Opening the phone book, she flipped through the pages till she found what she was looking for. Carefully, she addressed the envelope: Dominique's, Cedar Park Shopping Mall, Cedar Park, Illinois.

Then she ran upstairs to her room and went directly to the dresser. Pulling open a drawer, she rummaged through it until she found what she was looking for.

The silk scarf looked just as beautiful as it had the day Dana had given it to her. *Stolen* it for her more likely, Cassie thought. For the last time, she held it to her neck and admired her reflection.

Then, with only a small sigh of regret, she stuffed it in the envelope, sealed it, and put it in her purse. She'd mail it tomorrow.

10

No sooner had Cassie taken her seat in homeroom Monday morning than Alison came tearing in and plunked down next to her. Turning to face Cassie, her eyes wide and brimming with pity, she said, "Oh, Cassie, you poor thing. It must have been awful for you."

Cassie nodded solemnly. So far that morning she'd received three expressions of sympathy. She was beginning to feel like a poor, helpless victim—which wasn't so bad, really. It was better than being treated like a criminal.

"And you thought she was your friend," Alison continued.

"I did," Cassie said mournfully. "She wanted me to be her *best* friend, can you believe it? And all she really wanted was a . . . an accomplice."

"Wow," Alison breathed. "She's a regular juvenile delinquent. She certainly doesn't look like one."

Cassie nodded in agreement. "She sure had me fooled."

She saw Julie Bradshaw and Nancy Ellison looking at her, then huddling together in whispered conversation. "Do you think everyone knows it was Dana, not me, who took the blouse?" she asked Alison.

"Oh, sure," Alison assured her. "I called Amy and Susan yesterday and they're spreading the word."

The two biggest mouths in the Pep Club, Cassie thought. By now Dana's reputation should be totally wrecked. That was a comfort. Even so, Cassie glanced at the door uneasily. "I wouldn't want to be in her shoes today. Can you imagine how everyone's going to look at her when she walks in?"

"*If* she walks in." Alison sniffed. "If I were her, I wouldn't show my face within a mile of Cedar Park Junior High."

Cassie beamed at her. She was so lucky to have such loyal friends—especially after the way she'd ignored them when she was hanging out with Dana. She made a serious personal resolve to be a better friend from now on.

The bell rang and Cassie settled back. She tried to focus on the front of the room, but she kept shooting furtive glances at the door. She heard running footsteps coming up the now-empty hallway and quickly looked away.

But it wasn't Dana—it was Gary. She should have figured it couldn't be Dana. Dana would never run— she might muss up her hair.

Cassie patted her own hair as Gary came down the aisle toward his seat. But instead of taking his usual seat, right next to hers, he took an empty seat a couple of rows up. And he didn't even look at her.

He must not have heard what happened, Cassie thought. She'd tried to call him Saturday night, but the line had been busy. And when she'd tried Sunday, there'd been no answer.

As the teacher began calling roll, she debated her next step. She could wait and let him find out through the grapevine what had happened to her. Then he might feel guilty about being angry with her. Or she could tell him herself.

She ripped a sheet out of her notebook and started to scrawl a note: "Gary—could you meet me after school, at the side entrance? I have to talk to you."

Dimly, she heard the teacher calling names as she underlined *have* three times. "Baker" . . . "Here" . . . "Caldwell" . . . "Here" . . . "Cunningham . . . Cunningham?"

Cassie looked around and noticed a few kids exchanging meaningful glances. Someone giggled.

Serves her right, Cassie thought, examining her note. Still, she was kind of glad Dana wasn't there to see all this. . . .

The thought seemed to have come into her mind on its own. She frowned. What was she thinking? Dana deserved all the ridicule she would get after what she had done. Quickly, she wrote her name at the bottom of the note and folded it.

She was about to pass it up to Gary when she realized the teacher's eyes were on her.

"Cassie?"

"Yes?"

"I've called your name three times."

"Oh. Sorry. I'm here."

"So I see."

A couple of kids had turned and were grinning at her. Gary wasn't one of them. Oh, well—she'd get the note to him after class.

But when the bell rang, Gary darted out before she could reach his seat. Frustrated, Cassie gathered her books. He'd be sorry when he found out why she'd stood him up.

Maybe she'd find him at lunch. . . .

She came out of the cafeteria line half expecting to see Dana standing there with her fancy little lunch bag. She wasn't, and Cassie didn't see her anywhere in the cafeteria. Alison was right—Dana wasn't going to show her face.

Cassie spotted Barbie and Alison waving to her, and she headed toward them. It was such a good feeling, having friends saving a seat for you in the cafeteria. You knew you belonged. Poor Dana would never know that feeling. . . .

Once again, she frowned. Where did this "poor Dana" business come from? Dana didn't deserve friends.

"Want to go to the mall after school?" Barbie asked when she sat down.

"I don't think so," Cassie replied. "To tell the truth, I think I'd like to stay away from the mall for a while."

"Yeah, I see what you mean," Alison said. "Like, what

if you ran into someone from Connections? It could be pretty embarrassing."

Cassie shuddered. "Besides, I'm hoping Gary Stein will meet me after school. You know, I was supposed to meet him Saturday at the mall. Now he thinks I stood him up again."

Barbie was shaking her head. "Boy, that Dana really messed up your life."

"You're telling me."

"Hi, can we join you?" Cassie looked up and saw Julie Bradshaw and Nancy Ellison standing there, holding trays.

"Uh, sure," Cassie murmured, looking at Barbie and Alison in wonderment. They seemed pretty startled, too. The Debs had never sat at lunch with them before.

"We're just dying to know what really happened," Julie said as they sat down.

For the zillionth time, Cassie told her tale of woe. Julie and Nancy were a perfect audience, listening intently, nodding, and looking appropriately shocked at the right places.

"I knew it," Nancy said with satisfaction. "There was something very weird about that girl. She was awfully snobby for a new girl at school."

"I liked those pearls she wore," Julie mused. "I wonder if she stole them?"

"Probably," Barbie interjected. "Cassie, didn't you say she stole a scarf, too? And Lydia saw her take a lipstick."

Cassie examined her fingernails. "Well, yeah."

"She was such a show-off," Nancy commented, fingering the diamond pendant she always wore. "It's so tacky to go around telling people how rich you are."

"You know, her father's a very prominent business-man," Julie noted. "I thought they'd be invited to join the country club and Dana would be a Deb."

Nancy shook her head. "There's no way, now. Can you imagine the scandal if a Deb was caught shoplifting?"

"I heard you went to her house," Julie said to Cassie. "What was it like?"

"Big," Cassie said. "Lots of furniture. They've got a swimming pool and tennis courts in the back. And Dana's got a great room, with her own phone and TV and everything."

Nancy looked impressed. "If she's got all that, what does she need to steal blouses for?"

Cassie hesitated before speaking. "My Dad says sometimes kids do things like that because they have problems. He says we should feel sorry for her."

"Cassie!" Barbie exclaimed. "You're not standing up for her, are you?"

"Oh, no!" Cassie hastened to say. "But I'm just saying . . ." Her voice drifted off. What was she saying, anyway?

"I know what her problem is," Nancy said firmly. "She's a thief."

"And she tried to make Cassie look like a thief," Alison added.

Cassie had almost forgotten that part. "You're right," she said. "She's a thief. And a major creep." She picked at her food. "I wonder if she'll show up in Spanish?"

"Not if she's smart," Julie said. "If I were Dana, I'd transfer to another school."

Thinking about Spanish made Cassie think about

Gary. She looked around the cafeteria. He didn't seem to be there. Well, she'd catch up to him in class. . . .

Cassie entered her Spanish class tentatively. No Dana. But no Gary either. She took her seat, opened her notebook, and twiddled a pencil in her hand. Idly, she wondered where Dana was that very minute. Probably ripping off a gas station. . . .

Her head jerked up as Gary walked in. She watched him closely as he headed toward her desk. Had he heard anything yet? From the way he refused to look at her when he passed by, she figured he hadn't.

She reached into her pocketbook for the folded note, and turned to the person in back of her. "Pass this to Gary, okay?" Then she turned around and faced forward as the bell rang.

She barely heard the teacher that hour. Most of the time she was resisting the urge to look back at Gary to check out his expression.

Finally, class was over. Slowly, she jotted down the homework assignment while other kids jumped out of their seats and headed for the door. Taking her time, she gathered her stuff and started to rise. She was on her feet when Gary paused by her desk.

"Okay" was all he said before moving on.

Cassie hugged her jacket closer and hopped up and down. It was getting cold, and where was Gary? Was he going to stand her up, to teach her a lesson or something dumb like that?

Then she saw him coming down the steps. He wasn't exactly hurrying to meet her. When he finally reached her, he didn't say anything. He just stood there, waiting.

Cassie took a deep breath. "I want to tell you why I wasn't at the theater Saturday." Then, for the umpteenth-and-one time, she told her story.

At first he looked skeptical. Then he looked surprised. And finally, he looked horrified. "She *stole* a blouse?"

Cassie nodded. "And she tried to make me take the blame."

Gary whistled. "Wow. That's really wild."

They started walking away from the school. "I thought you two were friends," Gary said.

"I did, too," Cassie said, trying to sound sad and pitiful. "She betrayed me."

They walked in silence for a while.

"To tell you the truth," Gary said slowly, "I thought she seemed kind of conceited and stuck-up. What did you see in her, anyway?"

Cassie thought about that. What *had* she seen in Dana? Well, there were the great clothes, of course, and the glamorous travel. And the phone and the pool and the fancy house. . . . But for some reason, she didn't feel like telling Gary about that. She had a feeling he wouldn't understand. She wasn't even sure *she* understood.

"I guess I just thought she was interesting," she said lamely. "Look, can we not talk about Dana? Can we talk about something else?"

"Sure," Gary said. "Let's talk about going to a movie this weekend."

Cassie smiled happily. "That sounds good to me." She paused before adding, "As long as it's not at the mall."

11

OVER THE NEXT FEW DAYS, life seemed to go back to normal. Cassie was in her usual routine—classes, friends, the Pep Club—the routine she'd found perfectly satisfying before Dana had come into her life. And by Thursday afternoon, she'd almost managed to erase Dana's face from her mind.

There had been a particularly exhausting Pep Club meeting that afternoon. The members were still arguing over whether their new sweatshirts should be white with red letters or red with white letters. By the time Cassie got home, she wanted to collapse on her bed and spend the two hours before dinner recovering.

Then Daphne walked in.

"I was just wondering. . . ," she said slowly.

Cassie didn't bother to open her eyes. "Mmmm?"

"Have you seen Dana lately?"

"Huh-uh. She hasn't been at school all week."

She felt the bed bounce as Daphne sat down on the end of it. Reluctantly, she opened her eyes.

"Do you think she's sick?" Daphne asked.

"I don't know." Cassie raised herself up on her elbows. "How come you're so interested in Dana?"

Daphne looked troubled. "I was just reading the article from last Sunday's newspaper. You know, Dad's series on troubled adolescents. It reminded me of Dana."

Cassie hated to admit she hadn't read it, but now she was curious. "Why? What was it about?"

"It was about this girl who has anorexia nervosa. You know, the disease where you starve yourself."

"I know what it is. But Dana isn't starving herself."

"Yeah," Daphne murmured, "But the girl in the story made me think of Dana." She hesitated. "Maybe you should call her."

Cassie sat upright. "*Call her?* Why should I call her?"

Daphne shrugged. "She might really be sick or something."

"Then her housekeeper will call the doctor. *I'm* not going to call her."

"Call who?" Lydia bounded in and tossed her books on her bed.

"Daphne thinks I should call Dana because she hasn't been at school all week." Cassie made a face to show what she thought of that idea.

Lydia's eyebrows went up. "Really? She hasn't been in school at all? Maybe you *should* call her."

"Don't be ridiculous," Cassie said. "I am *not* going to call her."

119

"Then I'll call her," Lydia said.

"What?" Cassie jumped off the bed and followed Lydia out to the hall. "Why are you calling her?"

"If she hasn't been at school all week, there might be something really wrong," Lydia said. "What's her number?"

Cassie glared at her for a moment. Then, sighing, she gave her Dana's number. Lydia dialed and waited.

"There's no answer," she said, hanging up. "I think you should go over there and see if she's okay."

"Why don't you?" Daphne asked, looking at Cassie eagerly.

"You're both crazy," Cassie stated flatly, and went downstairs to the kitchen. Her mother was just coming in the back door.

"Wait till you hear this, Mom," Cassie told her. "Daphne and Lydia think I should go over to Dana's house to see if she's okay."

Lydia and Daphne were right behind her. "She hasn't been in school all week, Mom," Lydia said. "And her parents are probably away. And remember, she said the housekeeper never notices her."

Mrs. Gray appeared to be turning this notion over in her mind. "You know," she said finally, "that might not be a bad idea. Maybe I should go with you."

"No, I think it should be just me and Cassie," Lydia said. "If you come, it might freak her out. No offense, Mom."

"Hey, wait a minute," Cassie interrupted. "What's going on here? I have absolutely no desire to go over to Dana's."

"Oh, come on," Lydia urged. "Aren't you just the least bit curious about what's going on?"

Cassie paused. Actually, she *had* wondered about Dana—but she wasn't about to admit it. "Not really. Why should I care what happens to her?"

"Because she's a human being," Lydia argued.

"She's a very troubled girl," her mother added. "To be honest, I think she probably needs professional help. Maybe you kids could help her see that."

Cassie bit her lower lip. "It's my turn to set the table tonight."

"I'll do it for you," Daphne offered.

"Mom, will you give us a ride?" Lydia asked.

Mrs. Gray looked at the clock. "All right, but you'll have to walk home, okay?"

"Okay. C'mon, Cass."

Cassie couldn't believe this. One minute she was lying on her own bed, planning a nice nap before dinner; the next, she was in a car going to visit someone she'd sworn she never wanted to speak to again. How did she let herself get into this?

But deep in her heart of hearts, she had to admit she was a tiny bit curious. Not that she *cared* what happened to Dana. But it might be interesting to know what was going on, to have something to report back to the gang at school. . . .

"I'll wait and make sure you get in," their mother said as she pulled up in front of the mansion.

Lydia and Cassie got out and went to the door. Cassie rang the bell. "Why did you bring your backpack?" she asked Lydia while they waited. "We're not spending the night here!"

Before Lydia could answer, the same gray-haired woman Cassie had seen the other time she was there opened the door.

"Uh, hi, is Dana home?"

The housekeeper's eyes narrowed. "Who are you?"

"I'm Cassie Gray, and this is my sister, Lydia. I was here before, remember?"

"Yes, of course," the woman said vaguely. "Come in."

Cassie turned and waved to her mother as they walked inside.

"Dana is in her room," the housekeeper said. "She hasn't been out of it for days."

She waved her hand in the direction of the stairs, and the girls started to walk that way.

"I've sent for her mother," the housekeeper called after them ominously.

"Wow," Lydia breathed as they entered the upstairs hallway. "Do you know which room is hers?"

"I think it's this one," Cassie said in hushed tones. There was something about the house that made you want to whisper. Tentatively, she rapped on the door. After a few seconds, it opened.

Dana stared at them for a moment. Then she asked, "What are you doing here?"

Cassie glanced at Lydia, who was gaping at the inside of the bedroom. "Just wanted to see how you are," she managed nervously. Dana stepped aside and let them in.

She didn't look too good. Her hair was messy, and it needed washing. Her face was pale, and she was getting some spots on her chin. Her clothes—a rumpled sweat-suit—looked like they'd been slept in.

"I thought maybe you wanted to apologize," Dana said in a dull voice.

"Apologize?" Cassie shook her head. "I haven't done anything to apologize for. What you did was wrong, and you tried to stick the blame on me."

Out of the corner of her eye, she could see Lydia wandering around the room, looking at the TV and stereo. Maybe now she'd understand why Cassie had found Dana so appealing.

Dana sat down on the bed. "I would have explained all that if you'd given me a chance."

"Explained what?"

"Why I had to make it seem like you did it. See, they won't do anything to you if it's your first time. They just give you a warning."

Cassie's eyes widened. "You mean, you've been caught shoplifting before?"

Dana nodded. "That's why I got kicked out of my last boarding school. And I got caught in Chicago once."

From her tone, Cassie couldn't tell if she was ashamed or proud of this.

"Did they tell your parents?" Lydia asked.

"Sure," Dana said and uttered a short laugh. "My parents said I'd grow out of it." She was so nonchalant, she might have been talking about thumb sucking.

"Why do you do it?" Cassie asked. "I mean, you could buy anything you want. Why do you want to steal things?"

Dana just shrugged. Lydia sat down on the bed and looked at her intently. "You don't steal those things because you want them, do you? There's another reason."

Now Dana laughed out loud. "Are you trying to be a psychologist? I went to one of those guys once. What a jerk. He kept saying 'Why do you *really* want to steal?' Like I had some big weird secret."

Lydia opened her backpack and pulled out what looked like a bunch of newspaper clippings.

"What's that?" Cassie asked her.

"Articles from Dad's series," Lydia replied. "I thought maybe Dana might like to read them." She looked at Dana and smiled. "Maybe you'll see yourself in these."

Dana looked at her skeptically. "What are they about?"

Lydia examined one. "Well, this one's about a boy who's hooked on drugs."

"*I* don't do drugs," Dana said.

"That's not the point," Lydia murmured. "See, it turns out the reason he was taking drugs is because his parents were fighting and yelling all the time."

Dana's forehead wrinkled. "What does that have to do with me?"

"Well," Lydia said slowly, "sometimes people do things for reasons no one else knows. I mean, this kid didn't just want to get high. He wanted to escape from all the problems at home. Get it?"

"No," Dana said.

But Cassie had a feeling she knew what Lydia was saying. "You mean he didn't really like drugs—he was just taking them to get his mind off his real problems."

"Exactly!" Lydia exclaimed. "Now, this one is about a girl who has anorexia."

"Oh, lots of girls have that—it's no big deal," Dana said in a bored voice. "I knew a girl in boarding school

124

who had it. She was kind of chubby and she wanted to lose weight. But instead of going on a real diet, she starved herself."

Lydia held up the clipping. "But *this* girl, she didn't need to lose weight. She wasn't fat at all."

Dana looked almost interested in spite of herself. "So why was she starving herself?"

"She felt like no one at home paid any attention to her. So she thought if she stopped eating she'd get some attention."

For Cassie, it seemed as though pieces of a puzzle were coming together. The picture was becoming clear. "Your parents don't pay much attention to you, do they, Dana?"

"So what?" Dana asked sharply. "This way, I can do anything I want."

"I'll bet that's why you steal things," Cassie continued. "So you can get them to pay attention to you." She felt positively brilliant for figuring that out. And from the expression on Dana's face, she had a feeling she'd hit a nerve.

Dana's face distorted, and for a minute Cassie thought she was going to cry. She didn't, but Dana's next words were so soft Cassie could barely hear them.

"They don't care."

"How do you know that?" Lydia asked her in a voice that was unusually gentle for her. "Have you ever tried talking to them about it?"

"They're never here," Dana mumbled. "They wouldn't listen if they *were* here." Her voice got louder, and more bitter. "Do you think my father's going to let his business fall apart just to stay around here and listen to me? Do you think my mother's going to give up being on magazine covers?"

Poor Dana, Cassie thought. She thought about her own parents. Thank goodness they weren't like that.

She turned back to Dana. "Look, you've gotta at least *try* to talk to them."

"I'll bet they *do* care," Lydia said. "They just don't know how you feel."

Dana gave a small noncommittal shrug.

"And you should come back to school," Cassie said.

"And have everyone pointing at me and laughing? I'll bet you couldn't wait to tell them all that happened."

Cassie flushed. Maybe there was some truth in what she said, but . . . "I didn't have to tell them," she pointed out. "This is a small town. Word travels fast." Of course, she hadn't helped matters much. But maybe she could make up for that.

"People forget," Lydia said comfortingly. "I remember this girl in my class. She was out with some older kids and they took a car for a joyride. She got arrested and everything. But that was last spring, and now no one cares. In fact, she's on the Student Council now."

Dana was staring past Lydia, looking at nothing. Cassie couldn't get over how different she looked from that first day at school. She had seemed so glamorous then, so grown-up. Now she looked like a pathetic little kid, like an unwanted foster child, sad and lonely.

"We can help you at school," Cassie said impulsively. "You could hang out with me and my friends. When other kids see you with us, they'll know you're not so bad." She knew she wasn't putting it very well, but it was the best she could do.

Dana was silent for a few moments. Finally, she looked directly at Cassie. "About the blouse . . . I guess it *was* pretty bad, making you take the blame. I'm sorry."

"That's okay," Cassie said. "Well, no, it's not okay, but I forgive you."

"When's your mother coming back?" Lydia asked.

"Tonight."

"Are you going to talk to her about this?"

Dana drew her knees up to her chest and hugged them. "Maybe."

Well, at least she didn't say no. Cassie looked at Lydia.

"That's good," Lydia said. "It's a start." She turned to Cassie. "We better get home. It's almost time for dinner."

Cassie wrinkled her nose. "It's Thursday, right? That means meat loaf."

Dana got up with them. She seemed to be struggling for some words. "Uh, listen, you guys, um . . . thanks for coming." She looked at Cassie. Her face was wistful. "You're really lucky, you know? You've got nice parents, and all those sisters . . ." Her voice trailed off.

"I know," Cassie said. At least, now she did. "Will you be coming back to school?"

Again, Dana shrugged. "Maybe."

They paused at the door. Cassie touched Dana's shoulder. "Well, call me and let me know what happens, okay?"

"Okay."

Cassie and Lydia went out into the hall.

"Cassie?"

Cassie looked back at Dana. "Yeah?"

"I was just wondering . . . what's meat loaf?"

Cassie grinned at her. "Just come for dinner any Thursday night. You'll find out!"

12

"Fee, would you like another slice of pie?" Cassie asked.

Phoebe's eyes narrowed suspiciously. "Why?"

"C'mon, I know apple's your favorite. Why are you looking at me like that?"

"Because you're the one who's always telling me I eat too much. You said I should go on a diet."

Cassie laughed merrily. "Don't be silly, Fee. I think you're perfect just the way you are." She turned away from Phoebe's stunned expression to address the table in general. "Does anyone want more pie?"

"I'll have some," Lydia said, and turned to her parents. "It's really so sad about Dana. She's just like those kids in your articles, Dad."

"I wanted to cry, listening to her," Cassie said. "She

honestly doesn't think her parents care about her. It's like she's all alone in the world."

"That's awful," Daphne murmured. "Is that why she steals things?"

Cassie nodded. "I figured that out," she said proudly.

Mr. Gray turned to his wife. "I wonder if her parents even realize how they've neglected that child."

"Probably not," Mrs. Gray replied. "Although it's hard to believe they could be that blind."

"And I thought she was so lucky," Cassie said, shaking her head at her own foolishness. "I'd hate having parents like that." She bestowed her biggest and brightest smile on her parents. "I guess I've got about the best mother and father in the world."

Both her parents looked at her, their faces bearing the same expression Phoebe's had worn a few minutes earlier.

Cassie didn't care. She leaned back in her chair and smiled contentedly. Just looking around the table made her feel happy. Little Fee, with bits of apple on her chin . . . Daphne staring into space, lost in one of her daydreams . . . Lydia now lecturing about some cause or another—the best sisters in the world. And her parents, always there, always caring. . . .

She made a silent vow. From now on, no matter what, she'd be a good sister and a good daughter. She'd appreciate what she had, and stop whining for the things she didn't have.

Feeling terribly virtuous, she jumped up. "I'll clear the table."

"I think it's my turn, Cassie," Daphne said.

Cassie gathered some plates, and patted Daphne's shoulder as she passed her. "That's okay. You just sit there and think up a good poem or something."

Behind her back, she heard her father murmur, "What's going on?" Her mother replied, "Don't ask questions. Let's just see how long it lasts."

Silly parents, Cassie thought fondly as she stacked the dishes. They don't know that this is the way I'm going to be from now on, forever. She went back to the table for another pile, taking only a moment to flash them all an affectionate smile. She'd just returned to the kitchen when the phone rang. Quickly she set the dishes down and grabbed it. "Hello?"

"Is this Cassie?"

She knew the voice immediately. "Hi, Gary."

"Listen, I know we're supposed to be going to the movies on Saturday. But I just found out, I have to go to this party my cousin's having. He goes to Cedar Park High."

Cassie's heart sank. "Oh."

"Would you like to go with me?"

Talk about about speedy recoveries. A real high school party! "I'll have to ask my parents, but I'm sure it'll be okay. I'll let you know at school tomorrow, okay?"

"Great," Gary said. "See ya."

She practically floated back to the table. "That was Gary Stein," she announced.

Phoebe clapped a hand over her mouth. "Oh, I forgot to tell you—he called this afternoon."

It was on the tip of Cassie's tongue to scream something like "You imbecile—why didn't you tell me?" Then

she remembered her new resolve. Her dear little sister—
so what if she was a trifle forgetful? "That's all right,
Fee," she said sweetly, taking a second to enjoy the
astonishment on her face before turning to her parents.

"He wants me to go with him to his cousin's party
Saturday. His cousin's in the tenth grade. Can I go?"

Her father's forehead puckered. "A high school party?"

Cassie didn't like his tone of voice. She turned to her
mother. "Mom, *please?*"

"Find out if his parents are going to be there," her
mother said.

"If they are, can I go?"

Her parents looked at each other. "I suppose so," her
father said.

"Oh, thank you, thank you, thank you," Cassie gushed.
"I really have the best parents a girl could want."

"I can't deal with all this gratitude," Mr. Gray said.
"I'm going to start on the dishes." He got up and went
to the sink.

"Can I be excused?" Daphne asked. "There's something I want to see on television."

"What is it?" Cassie asked.

"A ballet. *Sleeping Beauty.*"

Yuck, Cassie thought. "Wouldn't you rather watch
music videos?" she asked hopefully.

Daphne shook her head. "No, I really want to see
this ballet."

For one brief, fleeting moment, Cassie thought of
Dana, who could watch anything she wanted, anytime
she wanted, on her own private television. But then,
Dana didn't have a sister like Daphne. You're the lucky

one, she reminded herself sternly. Of course, it was too bad she couldn't have a sister *and* a TV.

She thought about the party Saturday night. What would she wear? "Mom, can I get a new outfit for the party Saturday night?"

Mrs. Gray frowned. "We'll see. But it seems to me you bought some new clothes just last month."

Mentally, Cassie went through her closet and rejected everything in it. "But Mom, I need something more sophisticated. I don't want to look like a baby around all those high school kids."

"Cassie, I said we'll see."

Her father returned to the table. "What's going on?"

Cassie turned to him plaintively. "I want to get a new outfit for the party."

"And I said we'll see," her mother stated, annoyance creeping into her voice.

"But *Mom*—"

"Cassie! Stop whining!"

Cassie glared at her. Mrs. Gray glared right back. And Mr. Gray started laughing.

They both looked at him. Then Mrs. Gray started laughing, too. Cassie looked at them both in bewilderment.

"Well, it seems we have our daughter back," her father remarked.

"I knew it wouldn't last," her mother said.

Cassie rolled her eyes. "Okay, okay, I get the picture." She sighed dramatically. "I'm going to go look through my closet. There must be something in there I can wear. A rag, or something."

Oh, well, she thought as she climbed the stairs, nobody's perfect. No one could expect her to be completely nice all the time. At least she was trying. She ought to get some credit for that.

And who knows? If she was *really* nice, she just might get that new outfit after all.